HARTFORD PUBLIC LIBRARY

3 2520 10514 7010

D0630432

A King Production presents…

The *Bitch* *is* BACK **Part 3**

HARTFORD PUBLIC LIBRARY
ALBANY BRANCH
1250 ALBANY AVENUE
HARTFORD, CT 06112
695-7380

A Novel

DEJA KING

HARTFORD PUBLIC LIBRARY

This novel is a work of fiction. Any references to real people, events, establishments, or locales are intended only to give the fiction a sense of reality and authenticity. Other names, characters, and incidents occurring in the work are either the product of the author's imagination or are used fictitiously, as those fictionalized events and incidents that involve real persons. Any character that happens to share the name of a person who is an acquaintance of the author, past or present, is purely coincidental and is in no way intended to be an actual account involving that person.

ISBN 10: 0984332537
ISBN 13: 9780984332533
Cover concept by Deja King & www.mariondesigns.com
Cover model: Deja King
Cover layout and graphic design by: www.MarionDesigns.com
Typesetting: MarionDesigns
Editor: Linda Williams, Dolly Lopez and Suzy McGlown
Library of Congress Cataloging-in-Publication Data;
King, Deja

The Bitch Is Back a novel/by Deja King
For complete Library of Congress Copyright info visit;
www.joykingonline.com

A King Production
P.O. Box 912, Collierville, TN 38027

A King Production and the above portrayal log are trademarks of A King Production LLC

Copyright © 2010 by Deja King. All rights reserved. No part of this book may be reproduced in any form without the permission from the publisher, except by reviewer who may quote brief passage to be printed in a newspaper or magazine.

Printed in Canada

THIS BOOK IS DEDICATED TO MY:

Family, Readers and Supporters. I LOVE you guys so much.
Please believe that!!

3 2520 10314 7818

A PUBLISHER'S NOTE

Think of David vs. Goliath and yes the underdog won!! I've been in a vicious legal battle with Triple Crown Publications and Vickie Stringer for almost 2 years now. This fight has been draining on me and my family but I refused to lie down and let the wrong that had been done to me, defeat me! My mother once told me, "You have not because you ask not." I asked for it and it was delivered. I feel as if I stood up and fought for all the little people who are cheated, manipulated and done dirty in a cutthroat business. With faith and determination we shall continue to rise to the top! I feel blessed that the entire Bitch Series is under its rightful home, A King Production. I put my heart and soul into these books for my fans and now I know when I leave this earth my family can reap the rewards of my work. Soon I will upload video blogs to my website and Facebook page detailing my long legal journey and how I came to get the rights back to my books. Many said it couldn't be done but never underestimate one of God's children!! You know I had to share this because I LOVE my readers so much and I hope that I can prevent many of you from making some of the same mistakes I did. So please keep hope alive. If anybody in your life is doing you wrong, rebel and stand up for your rights. You will prevail!!

Hugs and Kisses from Your Literary Sweetheart!!

Joy Deja King

ACKNOWLEDGMENTS

Special Thanks To…

Linda Williams; You said it would happen and you were right!
You always believed in me and stayed true and loyal. That means
everything to me.

Jonesy; You were the first radio personality that embraced my
books! You set Bitch on fire in New York and I will forever love
you for that!! Now you can set it back on fire under A King
Production!! Kisses to you!

Tracy Taylor; Girl, you stay grindin' for the cause and be cute
doing it!

Ann Hopson; I see you girl… "You're so Pretty." ☺

Tazzy; I still adore you because I can always count on you being
you!!
Keith Saunders; You're my dude!! Enough said…

Book Bullies; I see you making ish happen in 2010!!

Tureko "Virgo" Straughter, Renee Tolson, Jeanni Dixon, Ms KiKi, Andrea Denise, Sunshine716, Ms. (Nichelle) Mona Lisa, Lady Scorpio, Travis Williams, Brittney, Donell Adams, Myra Green, Leona Romich, Sexy Xanyell. To vendors and distributors like African World Books, Teddy Okafor, Black & Nobel, DaBook Joint, The Cartel, LaQuita Adams, DCBookman, Tiah, Vanessa and Glenn Ledbetter, Junior Job, Anjekee Books, Andy Carter, Urban Xclusive DVD & Bookstore, Future Endeavors. Also, to Yvette George, Velva White, Carla Stotts and the rest of Diva's of Memphis, Devin Steel, Big Sue, Thaddeus Mathews, Sherita Nunn, James Davis, Marcus & Wayne Moody, Trista Russell, Don Diva and Dolly Lopez…thank you all for your support!!

Special, special thanks to Cover 2 Cover Book Club; Christian Davis, Angela Slater, Pamela Rice, Ahmita Blanks, Melony Blanks, Marcia Harvey, Melinda Woodson, Tonnetta Smith, Tiffany Neal, Miisha Fleming, Tamika Rice and Bar. I so enjoyed our book chats for "Hooker to Housewife" and "Superstar". All of you ladies are wonderful!!

DREAMS

Many say a dream is a premonition of what the future holds but as I fought the demons in my nightmare, I prayed that not to be the truth.

"Supreme, run! He's right behind you and he 'bout to bust off!" I screamed as I watched my husband beat the pavement, dodging bullet after bullet. It seemed the dark road he traveled never stopped and no matter how far his strides took him, it wasn't far enough to escape the danger behind him. I was frozen as I witnessed the final bullet penetrate in Supreme's back. He collapsed forward in slow motion. I felt life in my legs as I ran towards my husband, desperate for him to be alive, not wanting to lose him all over again. But the deliverer of his demise was now standing over him, sucking away Supreme's last breath by putting two more bullets in his head.

I immediately knelt down and held my husband for

what seemed to be the last time. It was déjà vu; back to when I thought he had been murdered right before my eyes in a bloody ambush outside of the hospital. Now it was happening all over again in my dream, and there was nothing I could do. The ski masked killer just stood there still aiming the heat at Supreme, dressed in all black and silent. As the tears continued to trickle down my cheeks, I leaped at him with blood drenched hands and ripped off his mask so I could stare into the eyes of the devil. I had to know who could be so cold as to take away my life for the second time. And my heart dropped as I faced evil… Pretty Boy Mike was back.

"Huh, huh, huh!" I jumped up in bed with my heart beating fast and gasping for air. My silk tank top and boy shorts were saturated in sweat as I awoke from my dream.

"Precious, are you okay, baby? This the fourth night in a row you've been having these nightmares," Supreme said stroking my hair.

"No, I'm not okay. I'm sick of seeing that sick fuck's face."

"Baby, Mike is upstate locked up. He's not going to hurt me or you."

"But my dreams seem so real. And that look in Mike's eyes keep haunting me. I can't shake his presence."

"You can't keep doing this to yourself. You were on the phone with me when I called the Clinton Correctional Facility. It's a maximum security prison and Mike ain't going anywhere. That man is on lockdown and will be for damn near the rest of his life."

"My ears hear you but my mind keeps telling me something else. And the thought of losing you again,

Supreme, is too much."

"That's why I want you to stop…"

"Aaliyah's crying. I have to go to her," I said ripping the covers from off of my thighs and stepping on the heated marble floor as I cut off Supreme mid-sentence. Supreme continued to speak but I had blocked off his words, only wanting to hold our daughter.

When I reached the hallway, Anna was walking up the stairs clutching a bottle in her hand. Although I appreciated the fact that Anna left her family in New York to continue running the household duties for me in Beverly Hills, I resented her caring for Aaliyah. She had grown so attached to our daughter, and it was only natural since she had become like a member of our family, but it still didn't sit well with me.

"Mrs. Mills, you didn't have to get up. I'll feed Aaliyah."

"Thanks, but no thanks, Anna. I can feed my daughter," I said, taking the bottle of warm milk out of her hands. "I'm sure you're tired. Go back to sleep."

"I'm fine. You go get some rest. I know you've had a long day. I can take care of the baby."

"I said I would do it." Anna knew from the tone of my voice that my decision wasn't negotiable. When I walked in Aaliyah's room and picked her up, she melted in my arms. I just held her close and rubbed her back, taking in her scent. Even though she was nine months old she still smelled like a newborn. I sat down on the rocking chair, ran my fingers through her jet black curls and watched as her tiny hands latched onto the bottle as she struggled to open her eyes, fighting the sleep. I gently caressed the side of Aaliyah's face. She greeted me with her sparkling green eyes that she inherited from my deceased mother who never had the opportunity to hold her only grandchild.

"My beautiful, Aaliyah, what did I do to deserve a daughter as precious as you?" Seeing my face and hearing my voice seemed to soothe her, because as fast as she opened her eyes she closed them and fell into a deep sleep. I removed the bottle from her mouth and laid her down in the crib. I gazed lovingly at the life I'd created before turning and walking out the door. But something made me stop and glance back at my daughter one more time.

I was overcome with this need to speak out loud as if Aaliyah could hear and understand me. "It was all worth it. Mike, the murders, the rape, it was all worth it just to have you in my life. Damn, I love you," I said.

When I returned to bed, Supreme was asleep and I laid my arm around his warm body, feeling blessed that I had so much more than what I had ever envisioned could be possible in my life.

Ring... ring... ring...!

"Supreme, get the phone," I mumbled, trying to not come out of my sleep. But the ringing wouldn't stop. I patted the space beside me and didn't feel the firm muscles of my husband's body. As the phone continued to ring I finally reached over and answered. "Hello."

"Precious, wake up, I need to speak to you."

"Who is this?"

"Girl, it's me, Maya. What other female would be calling you? You ain't got no friends."

"Maya, it's too early in the morning for bullshit. What is it?"

"It ain't that early."

I looked up to see the time and it was going on eleven o'clock. I couldn't believe I slept so late. Normally my day would start by eight a.m. because I would be awoken by Aaliyah's cries. I figured Supreme or Anna had fed Aaliyah and she went back to sleep since there was complete silence in the house. "Would you say what you want before I hang up the phone?"

"Damn, it's like that? Fine, let me break it down for you, since you acting salty. I believe that nigga, Clip is fucking around on me."

"Why?" I yawned trying to wake up.

"Because the mutherfucka didn't come home last night. I was blowing up his cell and he didn't pick up. When he finally brought his tired ass up in here, he gave me some lame-ass excuse about being in the studio all night."

"Maybe he's telling the truth. Did you check it out?"

"That's why I'm calling you. I want you to speak to Supreme and see if Clip was scheduled to be in the studio last night, and if so, what time did he break out."

"Maya, I ain't 'bout to get caught up in your bullshit and I damn sure ain't about to drag Supreme in it. That's his artist, they have a business relationship. Now you want me to put him in the middle of some juvenile nonsense. You gon' have to handle this shit with your man."

"I can't believe you. You supposed to be like my sister and you throwing shade in my game like this."

"Don't try to play those mind games with me, little girl. Now if you want me to do a drive by with you and we run up on that nigga catching him in the act, that's one thing. But I can't ask Supreme to be your detective and back track that man's studio time. That's some clown shit."

"Fine, I won't ask you to get Supreme involved, but I do want you to help me investigate. Ever since his single been blowing up the airwaves and now that his CD is about to drop, he's been on some ole extra fly shit. I use to let the bullshit slide, but now I feel like he being a tad over the top wit' it."

"Maybe you need to fall back. It's the summertime, school is out and you got a lot of extra time on your hands. Why don't you get a part-time job, take up a hobby or some shit? Dude probably ain't doing nothing but putting some finishing touches on his CD and you over there tripping."

"Man, please. If Supreme didn't come home last night you'd be driving up and down Sunset Boulevard with your nine in hand ready to blast off, so don't tell me to calm down."

"That's a different situation. We married with child. Speaking of Supreme, I do want to know where the hell he's at and to see Aaliyah. I'll call you back later on. But, Maya, don't go causing havoc over nothing. Trust, if Clip out in those streets doing dirt, the trash will come knocking at your front door more than happy to reveal all."

I hung up the phone with Maya and headed straight for Aaliyah's room. When I stood over her Bon Nuit Crib in Versailles pink, to my disappointment she wasn't laying there. I held up her boudoir pillow and cream cashmere blanket with crochet trim to inhale her scent. I then went downstairs and it was ridiculously quiet. "Is anybody here?" With no response, I walked through the sunken living room that opened up to the mosaic pool and hot tub. But there wasn't a face in sight. "Where the fuck is everybody at?" I hissed under my breath. I went back inside and picked up the cordless phone as I stood in front of the steel cased windows with frame jetliner views from downtown L.A. to Pacific Palisades, dialing Supreme's number.

"Precious," I heard Supreme belt out as I was about to hit the last digit.

"Where the hell were you, and where's Aaliyah?"

"Damn, let me at least close the front door, Can I get greeted with a kiss or something when I walk in the door and see my wife?" Supreme had his arms spread open as he stood in the forty feet high limestone entry.

"Of course you can get greeted with a kiss and a lot more from your wife," I teased and let my tongue tickle his earlobe. Supreme's hands traveled down my waist to my thighs, before gripping my ass.

"That's more like it. You need to let me slide in before I have to bounce."

"Where you going, and where's Aaliyah?"

"I left the new track this producer dropped off for Clip in my office. So I had to rush back here and pick up the CD before heading to the studio. Oh, and Anna took Aaliyah to the park. They left the same time that I did."

"You know I hate when Anna goes to the park with Aaliyah by herself. You should have gone with her or at least had one of your bodyguards posted up."

"You worry too much. They're fine. We're in Beverly Hills now, not crazy ass New York. Relax, just focus on me right now." I couldn't help but smile as Supreme, rubbed the tip of his nose against mine.

"You're right. I'm going to stop worrying and focus on you. I mean, you are sexy as shit. And standing here with all your muscles surrounding me is making a bitch thirsty. I know you're in a rush, but are you still trying to slide inside or what?"

"You don't even have to ask twice. Lead the way."

Supreme followed me up the sweeping double staircase and his hands remained cemented on my tiny waist. It was like after pushing out Aaliyah my body got even sicker; tits got perkier, ass got fatter and waist got tighter. And if I believed what Supreme said, my pussy even got wetter.

I guided Supreme's arms right past the two-sided stone and glass fireplace into our Phyllis Morris Cosmopolitan masterpiece. The sculpted Lucite and sparkling crystals mixed with platinum, silver and gold leaf finishes was the sort of bed that every hood queen dreamed of getting her back twisted out in, and I was no exception. Supreme had brought me to my highest level of satisfaction on this very bed on countless occasions, but something about the ambiance of this room always made it feel like the first time.

"Oh, daddy, you feel so damn good!" I purred as Supreme did tricks with his tongue in my sugar walls.

As my body got caught up in pure pleasure, my mind drifted to how luck was truly on my side. No longer was I on the grind on the brutal streets of New York. I was lying up in a palatial estate in Beverly Hills with my husband and our daughter, without a care in the world. When Jim Jones coined the term "ballin'" in his song, he had to be rapping about me.

"My pussy feels so on point," Supreme moaned as his manhood entered me. The thickness of his dick penetrating my insides snapped me out of my thoughts. As my nails sunk into the flesh of his back and my legs wrapped around his rock-hard ass I knew my life couldn't get any sweeter. "Baby, you've made all my dreams come true. You truly are my love for life," were the last words I echoed before losing my mind in his ecstasy.

RETALIATION

After Supreme laid that pipe on me right, I was feeling like a brand new woman ready to get up into some shit. But before heading out, I wanted to soak in our blue pearl hot tub. When Supreme and I placed our order at Advent Design, we straight tripped at how the company custom carved the tub from a block of specialty marble straight from Argentina. Hell, I had never even been to that part of the world, but if it looked half as good as how my deep saucer-shaped Ravenna tub felt, then I needed to book a flight.

I tilted my head back as the hot water seduced my body. The Jo Malone orange blossom scented candle intoxicated the air as I listened to Mary J. Blige. When I closed my eyes ready to fall into a daze, my cell phone started blaring. I ignored it at first, but whoever it was kept calling. Maya's name was flashing across the screen and I let out a deep sigh before finally answering. "Yes, Maya."

"Don't yes me. Why haven't you called me back?"

"Because I was getting crazy sexed by my husband and wasn't thinking 'bout yo' ass. That's why."

"Cute, but not funny. Are you still snuggled up wit' yo' man?"

"No, he had to go to the studio."

"Well then come over."

"For what, so I can hear you complain about Clip?"

"Please, Precious. This dude got me stressing."

"A'ight' let me put some clothes on and I'm on my way." I reluctantly stepped out of the tub and wrapped the cream Egyptian cotton towel around my body. When I stood in front of the floor-length vanity mirror, my heart dropped. There was Pretty Boy Mike standing behind me with a grin on his face, wearing the same outfit he wore the night he raped me: russet-colored pants with a cashmere V-neck sweater that fit perfectly on his six foot two frame.

I turned my head swiftly around the room searching for a weapon and when I swirled my head back around, Mike was gone. I turned on the faucet and splashed water on my face. I looked behind me again making sure my eyes weren't playing tricks on me. I hadn't thought about Mike in months, but lately I couldn't shake him and I couldn't understand why. I knew he was thousands of miles away, locked up on the East Coast, but for the last couple of weeks I felt as if the enemy was sleeping right next to me in my bed. I rushed to get dressed, desperate to get the hell out of the house.

I backed out the garage of our Mediterranean-style

mansion and pressed my foot down hard on the pedal of the black Bentley, a gift Supreme surprised me with last Christmas. My heart was still jumping out my chest as I drove past the tall iron security gates. I did eighty the whole drive, and by the time I reached the condo complex where Maya lived, my body was begging for a drink. I rang the doorbell and quickly became impatient when Maya didn't immediately answer. I then began banging on the door.

"Is the feds running up on you or what?" Maya joked, opening the door.

I brushed past her and hurried to the stainless steel bar in the corner space of the living room. I poured myself a double shot of Hennessey and relished in the burning sensation ripping through my throat.

"Precious, what the fuck is up with you?" Maya said, puzzled by my behavior.

"It's nothing. Can't a bitch be thirsty?" I said as I poured another shot. A chick like me didn't believe in sitting on nobody's couch and purging my soul to some therapist, but I was beginning to feel like I wouldn't have a choice if I couldn't stop shaking these Mike delusions. "So, what's going on with you and Clip?" I asked, trying to get my mind off of Mike.

Maya sat down on the couch rubbing her fingers through her asymmetrical black bob. I was still getting used to the new hair cut, but the shorter look definitely gave her a more sophisticated and mature appearance. "I believe that nigga seeing some sideline ho."

"Why, has the chick called you?"

"Not yet, but I feel it coming. He be sneaking and making calls and then hang up when I walk up on his shiesty ass. And when I check his phone, the numbers always be blocked. Then I found a bank receipt and he withdrew like thirty thousand dollars."

"I doubt Clip is hitting off some chick he fucking with that kind of paper."

"Well he damn sure didn't give it to me. I ain't seen no new pricey items coming through these doors. So who could he have given it to?"

"Did you ask him?"

"Nah, 'cause I don't want him to know I'm on to his bullshit. I'm trying to catch him out there to the point he can't deny the shit."

"Then what? You find out the nigga fucking around, are you gon' bounce or are you just gon' beef?"

"Man, I find out the muthafucka fucking around on me, talk about retaliation. This shit is gon' get brutal."

I put my glass down and sat across from Maya on the chaise. She was fidgeting with the zipper on her turquoise terrycloth jogging suit with venom in her eyes, ready for war. I knew that look because I had been there before. "Maya, I know you pissed, but sometimes the best retaliation is just walking away."

"Excuse me?"

"You heard me. The beginning of all the hell in my life started from wanting to retaliate against Nico. I found out he was fucking around on me with some hot-ass ho named Porscha and I lost my damn mind. I was relentless in my pursuit to bring that man down. My rage left a slew of dead bodies and brought about the murder of my mother and a very close friend, Boogie. Their blood will forever be stained on my hands. And don't forget about the death of my unborn child. So many lost lives, all for the taste of revenge. It ain't worth it, trust me."

"I hear what you saying, Precious, but what am I supposed to do, just let that nigga get away with it?"

"You don't even know if he's even doing anything. And if some foul shit is jumping off, either leave his ass or decide if he's worth fighting for. But please don't go down the path I traveled, because that shit turns serious real quick."

"Hold that thought," Maya said as she went to answer the phone. "Hello…hello? Stop calling my fucking house and not saying shit! Keep it up. I'ma put a trace on this damn phone, and when I find out who the fuck you are, I'ma beat yo' muthafuckin' ass!" Maya screamed before slamming down the phone.

"What the hell?"

"Oh, I didn't tell you about these fucking crank calls I've been getting for the last couple of weeks? This is another reason I'm mad suspicious. Like three times a day somebody calls and don't say shit. The number's private so I can't get no info. The bugged out part is that there is a block on this phone against private callers, but somehow this scandalous ho keep being able to get through."

"Maybe you should call the police."

"Bitch, what is you smoking?" Maya stared me down for a minute before continuing. "I can't believe you let that shit come out your mouth. You know we don't fuck with the police, they likely to find unregistered weapons, drugs or anything in this crib. I think living in that fairyland called Beverly Hills is starting to fuck your head up. Don't let that spectacular walled and gated Mediterranean villa you lounging in make you forget where you came from."

"Ain't nobody forgot where they came from. And who yo' young ass think you talking to all greasy like that? I can still bust yo' ass and anybody else who step in my way. Just because you getting some dick on a regular and you living with a man don't make you grown." Right when I was tempted to smack the shit out of Maya so she could remember who the fuck she was dealing with, Clip came staggering through the door, looking disheveled.

"Clip, what are you doing here? I thought you said you would be in the studio all day working," Maya inquired.

"I just came to get something," Clip said in an uneasy tone. He then turned and looked at me bug-eyed and said, "Precious, what you doing here?"

"Excuse me?" I questioned, taken aback since I came to see Maya on a regular.

"I mean, I didn't see your car outside so I just wasn't expecting for you to be here."

"I had to park on the other side of the building since there weren't any empty spaces when I pulled up."

"Why you looking all suspect, like you just robbed a bank or some shit?" Maya pried.

"Stop trippin'. I just got a lot shit on my mind," Clip responded, brushing Maya off.

"Well, that's what happens when you start trying to

stash some pussy on the low."

"Here we go. I ain't fucking around with nobody else. And do you really need to put all our business on front street?"

"Precious like my sister, I tell her everything. And she already knows what time it is."

"Well then, Precious, can you please tell your sister to stop harassing me over nonsense? I'm busting my ass in the studio every night so my debut CD can go multi-platinum and I can cop one of those estates my boss, Supreme got you living in."

"As long as you got me living up in those hills right along with you we won't have no problem," Maya popped with her hands crossed firmly across her chest.

"If you keep stressing me all the time with that bullshit, you gon' be living there before you know it. Except it won't be with me off my dime, but with Precious and Supreme."

"Fuck you!" Maya snapped, throwing a pillow across the room and hitting Clip in the back of the head as he walked to their bedroom.

"Yah, is some straight up clowns. But seriously, you need to think about what I said. Squash the drama before it even starts."

"I hear you, Precious, but a lot of times it's out of your control. Sometimes the drama finds you."

As what Maya said resonated in my head, my cell phone started ringing and it was Supreme. "Hi, baby, what's up?"

"Where are you?" Supreme asked with a hint of alarm

in his voice.

"At Maya's. Why, what's wrong?"

"I need for you to come home, now."

"Supreme, is everything okay?"

"I'll explain when you get here, just come home."
Then the phone went dead. I grabbed my purse in a panic.

"What did Supreme say?" Maya asked with a concerned look on her face.

"He told me to come home now. But it's not what he said, it's how he said it. Even though he was trying to sound like he was in control, I could hear underlying fear in his voice. He was definitely a tad shaky."

"I'm coming with you," Maya said, grabbing her keys. "Clip, I'm leaving with Precious. I'll call you later on."

Maya and I had slammed the door behind us before even waiting to hear a response from Clip. When we got in the Bentley and I put the key in the ignition, a flood of despair came over me.

THE NIGHTMARE BEGINS

When Maya and I pulled up to the gates, they were wide open. As I drove up to the entrance, we both noticed multiple police vehicles parked in front of the circular driveway. I couldn't get out the car fast enough, and sprinted to the front door. Maya was a step behind me when we entered the foyer. I zoomed in on the two middle-aged white detectives leaning against the keystone columns. I brushed past them, wanting to find Supreme so he could tell me what the hell was going on. I found him in his two-story office having an intense conversation with another detective who was writing down notes on a pad. "Supreme, what happened? Did someone break in and rob us?"

"Officer, this is my wife, Precious."

The officer reached out his hand to shake mine but my head was spinning into too many directions to care about formalities.

"Supreme, would you please tell me what the hell is going on?"

"Why don't you come sit down?"

"I don't want to sit down. I want you to tell me what the fuck is up," I said, becoming impatient.

"Mrs. Mills, it's concerning your daughter," the detective revealed calmly, unwilling to wait around for Supreme to build up the nerve to tell me.

"What about Aaliyah?"

"Your daughter's been kidnapped."

At that moment, time completely stopped. A painful chill infested every bone in my body, and my legs buckled. But before I lost my balance and fell, I grabbed onto the mahogany desk for support. Supreme put his hand on my shoulder, but I jerked it away. I ran out the room and I heard Supreme and Maya calling my name, but I ignored them. I had to find the person who could give me real answers instead of listening to someone ask me a million questions. As the stiletto heels of my Jimmy Choo shoes clicked against the marble floor and echoed through our twelve thousand square foot domain, I found who I was looking for, sitting on a chair in the kitchen, with an ice pack on the back of her head. "What happened to Aaliyah?" I demanded to know from Anna.

"Detective, this is Mrs. Mills, Aaliyah's mother."

"Hello, I'm Detective Moore. I'm sorry about your daughter. I was going over with your nanny exactly…"

But before he could continue with his bullshit apology, I was in spitting range of Anna's face. "What did you do to my baby?"

"Mrs. Mills, I didn't do anything. I turned around for less than a second, and then someone hit me on the back of the head. I blanked out for a few minutes, and when I came to, someone had grabbed Aaliyah from her stroller. I'm so sorry, Mrs. Mills."

As if on auto pilot, my hands found there way around Anna's thick neck and I couldn't let go. My grip was secure, and the fear in Anna's almond brown eyes made them bulge. "Tell me what you did to my daughter!" I kept repeating, not caring that I was committing murder right in front of a police detective. I watched as the color drained from her olive colored skin. I knew at that moment Anna wished that she'd kept her ass in Washington Heights with her family instead of following me to California, and so did I.

"Precious, let her go!" I heard Supreme bark.

The detective's hands were latched onto my arms trying to break my grip on Anna, but my anger had given me superhero strength. It took the detective, a police officer and Supreme to pry me away from Anna. When she was finally free from my clutches, she fell to the floor gasping for air, but I didn't give a fuck. Unless she could miraculously bring my daughter home to me at that very moment, she could choke on the floor and die for all I cared.

"We're going to have to place your wife under arrest," the police officer said, holding my hands behind my back.

"Please don't. My wife's in shock," Supreme pleaded.

"Officer, I don't want to press any charges against Mrs. Mills," Anna begged, coughing between words. The detective brought her some water as she sat back down on the chair finally catching her breath.

"I understand you're upset, Mrs. Mills, but this is a tragedy and it's nobody's fault except for the person who kidnapped your daughter. Resorting to violence against the nanny isn't going to make things better. If anything, it will make it worse, especially for you. Under the circumstances, I won't place you under arrest, but you have to get a hold of yourself. The only thing we all should be focusing on is bringing your daughter home safely."

I heard what the officer was saying, but it meant nothing. I felt as if the walls were closing in on me and I was suffocating. This was worse than any dream I had the past couple of weeks. This was a nightmare that I would sacrifice my own life to get out of, if doing so would guarantee that Aaliyah would be safe and live a long and prosperous life.

"What do we do next?" I finally asked, needing to believe that some sort of plan was being put in place to bring my daughter home alive.

"We have a couple of witnesses that saw a woman running, carrying a baby in her hands, and then driving off in a black four-door sedan. One of the witnesses was able to get a partial license plate number and we are doing our best to track the car down. We're also installing a device to your home phones because we believe the kidnappers will be calling demanding a ransom. Your husband is a very high-profile celebrity, and more than likely someone is looking for a quick payday. Whoever did this has probably been watching your family for some time now. From what I understand, Anna would take your daughter to this park frequently. They probably knew she would be alone and vulnerable."

"Did anybody get a good look at the woman who was running off with Aaliyah?" I asked.

"She was wearing a dark baseball cap, and either was a Hispanic or a light-skinned medium-built Black woman. It's not much, but it gives us something to go on."

"Do you believe she was acting alone or had help?" Supreme questioned, wrapping his arms around me, doing his best to make me feel safe.

"None of the witnesses mentioned seeing anybody else in the car, but normally with kidnappings, the perpetrator is not acting alone. So I wouldn't be surprised if someone else is involved."

While Supreme continued to talk with the detective, I freed myself from his clutches, making my exit. I walked outside and sat down on a chair by the pool, gazing into the tranquil clear water. The sun was setting and a glimmer of light was hitting the sculpted water fountain in front of the gazebo. Who would ever believe that in this majestic estate of glamour and opulence a dark cloud would come over and suck all the life right out?

"Precious, I promise it will be okay," I heard Maya say, intruding on my space.

"Maya, I really want to be alone."

"I know that's what your mind is telling you, but if you listen to your heart it's saying something else."

"Yeah, it is. It's saying that when I find out who had the fucking balls to snatch my daughter, I'm going to take pleasure in slowly cutting out their heart and watching them bleed to death. But until then, I want to be alone."

"I'll let you be, for now, but if you need me, call me. I'll be back tomorrow to check on you."

As Maya turned to leave, Supreme came walking up, and I put my head down not wanting to speak with him either. "Baby, it's getting late, let's go inside."

"Supreme, just like I told Maya, I want to be alone. So just go."

"Don't shut me out. I'm your husband and Aaliyah is my daughter too. I'm hurting just like you are. We have to be there for each other."

"Then why weren't you there for Aaliyah?"

"Precious, I know you're not blaming me for this. First Anna, now me."

"You knew I couldn't fucking stand for Anna and Aaliyah to be at the park alone."

"They weren't alone, it's a fucking public park. Lots of other kids and their parents were there too."

"That's not the point. Those other people don't live our lives. Would it have been so difficult for you to have one of your bodyguards be with Anna when she would go out with Aaliyah? Fuck...shit...damn!" I repeated, holding my head down and fighting back the tears that were moistening my fingertips. "If only you had listened to me, Aaliyah would be here right now. I would be holding her, feeding her, getting her ready for bed. Instead, I'm sitting here disgusted with you."

"Don't do this. Don't let that fucking sick monster, who took our baby destroy us too. We better than that, Precious."

"I don't know. If I don't get my daughter back, I don't know what's going to happen to me, or what's going to happen to us."

"We will get her back. You have to believe that. I put that on my life," Supreme said, pounding his fist into the palm of his hand.

"I have no choice but to believe you, because honestly, that's the only thing keeping me sane right now." I left Supreme sitting by the pool and went upstairs to take a shower. Being near him was too painful. I didn't want to, but part of me did blame Supreme and the other part blamed Anna. Deep down inside I knew it wasn't either one of their faults, but I had to blame somebody in order to stop myself from going crazy.

I stripped out of my clothes ready to baptize my body in the hot water when I heard my cell ringing. I realized my phone was in my purse, and when I reached in to get it a blocked number came across the screen. "Hello."

"I missed hearing your voice."

"Who is this?"

"You know who it is. Have you missed me as much as I missed you?"

I swallowed hard, feeling as if I was about to vomit up blood. I remained silent, unable to speak.

"Precious, it's extremely impolite to ignore my question. You can't be surprised to hear from me."

I still couldn't speak.

"Well, I have to be going, but before I do, someone wants to say hello." There was a pause and then the male voice said, "Say hello to your mommy," and I heard the cries of a baby-my baby. That bastard had stolen my child.

"You sonofabitch, bring my daughter home or I swear I going to cut your fucking dick off!"

"Some things never change. You still have that lethal mouth. But that's one of the many things I find so irresistible about you. But listen, I must be going. I think it's only fair I make up for the many months I lost and start spending some quality time with my daughter. She really is a beauty. I'll be in touch."

I dropped the phone, as I stood in the middle of the room butt naked with my mouth wide open, still in shock.

"Precious, who was that on the phone?" Supreme asked, standing in the doorway.

"He has her. He has Aaliyah," I revealed in a monotone voice.

"Who?" Supreme demanded, coming towards me. He grabbed my arms and asked again, trying to shake me out of my hypnotic state. "Who has our daughter? Tell me!"

"Mike."

"Who?" he asked again, not registering what I was saying.

"Pretty Boy Mike is back, and he has my baby!"

DELUSIONAL

"Mike is locked up, he's in jail. Stop with this bullshit!" Supreme yelled, while grabbing my cell phone. "Fucking blocked number," he said, scanning my call history. "I'ma see if the cops can put a trace on this."

"I know Mike's voice and I know the sound of my own child. That sick fuck has Aaliyah, and I'm getting her back. I don't give a damn what you think." I picked up the jeans and shirt I just threw off and started putting them back on.

"This is bananas. I'm going to prove to you that there is no way Mike has Aaliyah."

"And how do you plan to do that?"

"I'm going to have the detective call the prison and verify that Mike is still locked up. When that's done, I want you to stop this obsession with Mike."

"So what, you think I'm crazy and I just made up the whole conversation I had with Mike?"

"I'm saying that you're under a lot of stress right

now, which is understandable. It's probably leaked out that our daughter has been kidnapped and some loco is fucking with your head."

"You can't be serious with that lame-ass excuse. Talk about reaching; the only part of your explanation that's correct is some fucking loco is playing with my head, but his name is Mike."

"If the detective can get a hundred percent verification that Mike is still locked up at the Clinton Correctional Facility will you let it go?"

I knew I wasn't crazy, but I also knew that it was humanly impossible for someone to be two different places at the same time. If it was proven that Mike was locked down, then I had to get over it and focus my energy on finding the real culprit. "Yes, if Mike is still at Clinton, then I'll let it go." With that, I followed Supreme downstairs to speak with the lead detective on the case. The crowd had dispersed and only a few officers were still lingering around.

"We haven't gotten any new leads," Detective Moore said before we even had a chance to get out one word.

"Well, I have a lead. I know exactly who took my daughter. His name is Mike Owens."

Supreme eyeballed me with a mixture of annoyance and anger in his eyes but I could care less. I knew I was right and didn't need him to co-sign.

"Who is Mike Owens, and where can we locate him?" Detective Moore asked, and grabbed a pen out of his pocket, anxious to take down the new information.

"He's at the Clinton Correctional Facility in upstate

New York," Supreme was quick to make clear.

"Excuse me, I'm confused." The detective flipped his pen on his pad waiting for clarification.

"See, Mike is a madman..."

"I got this, Precious," Supreme interrupted, putting his hand up to let me know to chill. I didn't appreciate his attitude and wanted to knock him upside the head, but decided to let him give his two cents. The sooner the detective could prove that Mike had somehow been released or escaped from prison, the faster everyone would believe he was the one who had Aaliyah kidnapped. I waited impatiently as Supreme gave the detective the spill of our past dealings with Mike up until now.

"So Mrs. Mills, you claim this Mike character called you a little while ago?"

"Yes, it was from a block number, but I'm hoping you can still have the phone company put a trace on the call."

"That shouldn't be a problem. I'll just need your phone number and the carrier. What did the caller say?"

"Mike asked if I missed him, and said someone wanted to say hello. That's when I heard Aaliyah's voice."

"That could've been any baby's voice."

"Supreme, like I told you before, I know the sound of my own child's voice." It was taking all my strength not to lash out at my husband, but Supreme was wearing down my last nerve by not believing me. I could see if I was some delusional crackhead off the corner that he didn't know from Adam, but I was his fucking *wife*. That should've been enough proof right there.

"Mrs. Mills, did Mike say anything else?"

"Only that he had my daughter and he would be in touch." I decided there was no point in mentioning that Mike believed he was Aaliyah's father. To me, at this point it was irrelevant and wouldn't help the police track down Mike any sooner. Plus, all it would do was cause even more tension between me and Supreme and I couldn't deal with that right now.

"Okay, well I'm going to make a few phone calls and find out if this Mike Owens guy is still locked up. I'm also going to put a trace on that call you received."

"Trust me, Detective, you'll see Mike is no longer at Clinton. He has Aaliyah and you need to get your men on it immediately. He might still be in California."

"I understand your concern and frustration. We've already issued an Amber Alert. I promise if Mike Owens is our man, we will bring that bastard down. Now let me make these calls."

I turned and walked towards the living room and sat down on the couch. I was anxious for the detective and Supreme to realize I was right. Time wasn't on our side, and the sooner everyone acknowledged Mike was buried deep in this shit, they could focus their energy on him. I buried my head in my hands replaying my conversation with Mike over and over again.

From the corner of my eye I could see Supreme walking towards me. He sat down next to me and put his hand on my shoulder. "Precious, I know you believe that Mike is the one that has Aaliyah. But when the detective comes back and tells you he's still locked up, you have to promise me you'll stop. This isn't healthy for you and it's not going to help bring back our daughter."

"I have no problem making you that promise because I know I'm right. You'll see the detective is going to find out that Mike is free. And then maybe you'll apologize for not believing me."

Supreme and I sat in silence for at least an hour waiting for Detective Moore to give us an update. I was becoming so restless that I began pacing the floor. I needed a drink but decided against it, wanting my mind to stay clear and centered.

I practically jumped across the room when I noticed the detective coming in our direction. I stepped forward in front of Supreme, wanting to be vindicated. "I was right, wasn't I? Mike is out." I rolled my eyes at Supreme, pissed at his ass for not believing me.

"Actually, Mrs. Mills, Mike Owens is still locked up at the Clinton Correctional Facility and has been there since being found guilty of attempted murder against your husband and raping you."

"There has to be a mistake. Mike called me and he had my daughter."

"It just isn't possible. The warden even went so far as to have a guard go to his jail cell to guarantee he was physically there. The phone company is still tracing the number that called you, but I believe your husband is probably right and some disturbed creep thought he'd get a kick out of playing a sick joke on you. It happens. I'm sorry, but at least we can cross Mike off our list and move on to other possible suspects."

"I appreciate you getting to the bottom of this, Detective

Moore." Supreme stood up shaking the detective's hand. "Please keep us informed of any new developments. I'll also have my people working on any leads."

"I will be in touch, and again, we will do everything possible to bring your daughter home."

I watched in shock and confusion as the detective and the other officers left our house. My mouth remained open, and in my head I was screaming like a mad woman but nothing was coming out. "How could I have been so wrong?" I finally said.

"Baby, it's not your fault. You're vulnerable right now and someone is playing with your emotions. Whoever it was will be shut down, but right now we have to concentrate on finding who kidnapped our daughter. And Precious," Supreme paused and lifted up my chin so our eyes locked. "We have to remain strong and remember that we love each other. Nothing can change that. In the course of our relationship, we've been through so much bullshit and made it with chins up, and we'll do the same with this shit too. But you have to trust me and listen to me. If I have to shut down every fucking state, I will bring our daughter home." Supreme wrapped his arms around me and his embrace did make me feel secure, but it didn't shake the lump in the pit of my stomach.

That night I watched as Supreme fell into a deep sleep. Unlike him, I kept tossing and turning replaying the conversation I had with the would-be Mike imposter. The thing was, in my mind it wasn't an imposter. The tone, word selection and vibe all spelled out Pretty Boy Mike to me, and nothing or no one could convince me otherwise.

I glanced at the clock and it was two o'clock in the morning. I then looked back at Supreme and realized that I could either follow my husband's lead and live with the possibility that I would never see my daughter again, or I could follow my gut and handle it my way.

FULLY LOADED

"Please buckle your seatbelts as we prepare for landing," the pilot announced as the plane began descending into the Newark, New Jersey airport. I closed my eyes, mentally checking off everything I had to do in order to get to the truth. Following my gut had the distinct possibility of taking me on a tumultuous journey. But weighing the odds, I didn't have a choice.

After the flight landed I headed straight to the Enterprise Car Rental window. While waiting in line, I turned on my cell phone and checked my messages. There were a couple of voice messages from Maya and a ton from Supreme, not including the text messages he sent. I knew he would be furious to wake up and see that I was gone, but I had no choice. While deleting the fourth repetitive message from Supreme, my phone began ringing and it was him. I debated whether to take his call, but I didn't want him stressing, wondering if I was safe or not so I answered. "Hi," I said calmly.

"Hi is all you have to say? Where are you?"

"Handling some things."

"Things like what?"

I could tell by the tone of his voice that he wanted to explode on me but was trying to keep his cool. "It's complicated. But once I got it figured out I'll let you know what's up."

"Nah, that's not going to cut it. I wake up in the morning thinking my wife is going to be lying next to me and you're gone. Our daughter has been kidnapped, we're caught in the middle of a disaster, and you wanna break the fuck out?"

"Supreme, calm down."

"Don't fucking tell me to calm down. I've been calling you since eight o'clock this morning and your phone is going straight to voice mail. It's six or seven hours later and you want to call me back talking about you out handling some things. You 'un lost your damn mind. This shit is unacceptable. I want to know where you are right now."

"Supreme, my phone is going out. I'll call you back." I pressed the end button and turned my phone off. Having a long, going nowhere conversation with Supreme was too distracting. I was on a mission and wasn't going to allow not even my husband to sidetrack me.

After signing off on the paperwork, I got in the rented SUV and headed to the storage facility I still kept in Jersey City. When Supreme and I left the East Coast to start a new life in Cali, you would've thought I'd sever all ties to my past, but I couldn't bring myself to let go. I still kept money, a couple of weapons, clothes, pictures and other important items I took from my mother's house after she was killed. The warehouse represented my connection to my past, and for some reason I knew I would be back.

Eyeing my watch once again, time wasn't on my side. When I got to the storage spot I grabbed two stacks that totaled twenty-five thousand, pulled out the nine, made sure it was fully loaded and broke out. I then hit the FDR and made a pit stop in Harlem to purchase a burner to make all my phone calls. In no time I was driving over the Brooklyn Bridge to pay an old friend a visit. When I pulled up to the corner of a quiet working class block in the Bushwick section of Brooklyn, I turned off the truck and waited patiently.

Less than thirty minutes later, still maintaining the same schedule after all this time, my old friend came walking up the street carrying one bag of groceries, and headed into a modest brick two-story home. I waited ten minutes before getting out and knocking on the front door.

"Who is it?" the pleasant voice asked through the door.

"It's me, Precious."

"Precious, Precious who?"

"Precious Cummings." I heard the top lock being opened and the chain unclamped.

"Precious, is that really you?" Ms. Duncan greeted me with bright eyes when she saw my face. "Child, I ain't seen you in forever. Come in this house and give me a hug."

Seeing Ms. Duncan and feeling her arms around me gave me a brief moment of solace. This was the woman who would care for me sometimes when my mother was out pulling tricks. She was also the woman I trusted to make sure my mother had a decent burial when I felt it wasn't safe for me to show my face in Brooklyn. She had been one of the few people in my life that I felt I could count on without stabbing me in the back. That's what brought me to her front door, because I needed her help.

"Yes, it's been a long time but here I am."

"Look at you, still pretty as ever." Ms. Duncan gently grabbed my hand and led me into her cozy living room. Her floral couches were surrounded by a wall-length bookcase full of paperbacks and hardcover books. An elongated reddish wooden desk full of family portraits, cards that she'd gathered all through the years and desktop ornaments with passages from the Bible inscribed on them sat on the other side of the room. I knew that Ms. Duncan was a God fearing woman, but like most who came from poverty and had family members who hustled, she understood the struggle of the streets, and that's why we were always able to see eye-to-eye.

"It's so good to see you. How have you been, and how in the world did you find me?" Ms. Duncan was sitting across me, and by the gleam in her eyes I knew she had a million questions for me.

"I did some asking around and was told you no longer lived in the projects I grew up in and was now living in a house over in this area."

"Yeah, my mother passed away last year and she left me this house."

"I'm so sorry to hear that."

"Don't be. We weren't close for many years. When

she got remarried, her husband didn't want nothing to do with me and my brother. Then after he died, she reached out to us. My brother was still bitter and didn't want anything to do with her, but I had forgiven her and we were able to find closure before she died."

"I'm glad to hear that." I was trying to be serene with Ms. Duncan, but under my current circumstances, hearing about her dead mother wasn't on the menu.

"Oh, child, enough about me," Ms. Duncan said, swinging her arm midair. "Last I heard you were married to some famous man and that you had a baby. Is that true, because you know I don't hardly watch any television or read the newspaper? It's always so much violence going on and I try my best to tune it out."

"It's true, but I don't want to talk about them right now." If I didn't cut to the chase, I knew Ms. Duncan would be having a catch-up-on-the-past conversation with me for hours, and again that just wasn't on the menu. This visit was about me and what I wanted.

"What can I do for you?" she asked, as if reading my mind.

"Listen, I no longer have any connections in the streets. They're either dead, in jail or missing. I need to be hooked up with a person who can get me some fraudulent documents that look official, and I need them tonight. You have to know somebody still in the game that you can trust because I don't have anybody to turn to for help but you."

"Precious, are you in some type of trouble?"

"Trouble is an understatement. This is life or death." I wanted Ms. Duncan to completely comprehend that this situation was dire. Although the way I posed the question, it seemed as if I was asking for her help. In actuality, I was demanding it, but I hoped the subtle approach would be effective because I didn't want shit to get ugly. See, not only was Ms. Duncan's son a repeat felon, her younger brother was well connected in the streets. He even somehow managed to never do any serious prison bids, only doing short stints a couple of times for minor traffic violations.

"I know if you've come to me you have no other way out. So I'll do whatever you need." Ms. Duncan rested her smooth coal-colored hand on top of mine as if trying to send a blessing through me. But the only blessing I wanted was that of a connect. "I'm going to place a call to my brother, Ricky. He can get anything done. I can also trust him to be discreet," she added.

"I appreciate this. And you know I'm going to make sure you're taken care of for looking out for me."

"You've always been good to me. Just for making the funeral arrangements for your mother, you gave me all that money to show your appreciation. Because of your generosity, I was able to keep my grandkids fed and clothed while their father was locked up and their mother was somewhere doing... hell, I don't even want to think about it. So if I can repay the favor, then it soothes my heart."

I sat back and listened as Ms. Duncan picked up the phone and called her brother. I took a deep breath, trying to calm my nerves and maintain my sanity while my insides were slowly dying. Being proactive and conducting my own investigation instead of waiting on the police to break the case was the only thing that was keeping me sane. I was never one to leave my destiny in another person's hands, and I damn sure wasn't about to do it with the most precious person in my life.

"Here." Ms. Duncan handed me a piece of paper with an address written down. "Ricky, said for you to meet him there in an hour."

"Thank you."

"Of course, you've always been special to me, Precious. Ricky is going to take real good care of you. If you need anything else, you know where to find me. I'll always be here for you—I mean that."

I nodded my head, not wanting to say too much. I could feel tears struggling to swell up in my eyes, but I refused to give in. I swallowed hard, fighting them back.

"If you want to tell me what's going on in your life that's causing you so much pain, I'll be more than happy to listen."

"Maybe another time. I really need to go." Before opening the front door this overwhelming need came over me and I turned back to face Ms. Duncan. "Would you please pray for me and my family?" I was never one to get down on my knees and beg God for anything. I got by in life with the belief that you don't wait for things to happen; you make them happen. It seemed to pretty much work for me, but at that moment something inside of my soul was moved to ask that of Ms. Duncan, because the battle I was about to fight needed more than just me. It required the blessings of a higher power.

"That's all I've been doing since you sat down on

that couch." Ms. Duncan gave me a sincere smile and I walked out of her house.

When I arrived at a warehouse on a desolate stretch of Fountain Avenue, I hesitated to pull into the unpaved parking area. I took out my nine millimeter from the glove compartment, feeling uneasy. Ms. Duncan wrote down her brother's cell number on the paper so I dialed it to double check that I was at the correct location. Right then, I noticed a silver Lincoln driving up beside me flashing its high beams. I lifted up my gun ready to blast through the car's passenger window until the driver side door opened and a man who looked to be in his early forties stepped out. He had the same smooth coal complexion and big bright eyes as Ms. Duncan.

"I'm Ricky. You must be Precious."

I lowered my gun and relaxed. "That's right."

"Park your car and follow me inside."

What looked to be an abandoned warehouse on the outside was a meticulously clean, fully carpeted mini pad on the inside. There was a full stocked bar with bar stools greeting you when you first entered. On my right side there was a round table and chairs, with playing cards and stacked chips, which were obviously used for gambling. To the far left there was a complete black leather living room set with a sixty inch plasma television mounted on the wall.

"Would you like a drink?" Ricky asked as he deactivated one alarm and activated another.

"No, I'm good."

"Then let's do this."

I followed Ricky to a bedroom in the back that had a door leading to another room that looked to be an office. He then hit a button on his key chain that activated the six-drawer chest against the wall, which shifted to the side to reveal a staircase leading to the basement. The set of steps led to a criminal's paradise. Without question, he had his operation on a tight leash, which explained why he never got caught and had to do some serious time. Unless you made it down the stairs, you would think that at the most he was running an after-hour spot, nothing of this magnitude. On one table there was an array of guns, anything from AK-47s to Mac-10s. On another table was a pharmaceutical heaven, from prescription drugs, ecstasy, cocaine, heroin, and drug paraphernalia. Then there were high tech computers, tons of machinery that I assumed were used to make counterfeit money, and whatever else he needed.

"Your sister was right when she said you can get anything done. You have some serious shit popping off down here."

"Yeah, and honestly I would've preferred not to bring you down here since only a handful of people have seen all this. But my sister said you were like family to her and you needed some documentation today. With short notice like that I didn't have a choice but to bring you right here where the magic happens and get it done."

"So that's what some of these machines are for?" I asked, looking at them carefully.

"You damn right. I have the exact same equipment the big dogs use to manufacture whatever documentation is required to get clearance anywhere. My packaging is so clean that it would probably pass intense scrutiny from the Central Intelligence Agency."

"Now we talking, because I need the proper credentials to get inside a maximum security prison."

"Which one?"

"Clinton Correctional Facility."

"Over there in Dannemora?"

I nodded my head yes.

"They call that New York's Siberia due to the cold and isolation. You know everybody from Tupac Shakur, Ol' Dirty Bastard to Joel Rifkin, who is still locked up, has done time there. Their security is top of the line. I hope you're not trying to break anybody out, although for the right price it can be done." Ricky gave me a charming smile, letting me know not to underestimate his skills.

I couldn't help but laugh to myself imagining the games he probably ran around women his age and much younger. Even in his forties he was maintaining his playboy form. With a well-built six-one frame, neatly trimmed edges highlighting his waves, handsome face that still wasn't showing any signs of stressful living, and grown man clothes that consisted of tailored slacks, tucked in shirt with a belt accentuating a preserved waist and manicured hands, his appearance was as tightly put together as his illegal operations. "No I'm not trying to break anybody out. In fact, I'm going to confirm that somebody is still in and that he won't be getting out."

"I take it he isn't a friend of yours. What's his name?"

"Michael Owens. Why?"

Ricky went over to one of his computers and began

typing in some information.

"What are you doing?"

He put up his finger motioning for me to wait. "The stats on here indicate that he's still locked up and has many more years to go before he'll have a chance to see the light of day."

I stood next to Ricky to see the screen he was getting his information from. "Are you accessing the prison system?"

"This is much more detailed. I've accessed the personal files of Clinton's prisoners. You see right there," he pointed to Mike's name. "I click on his name and all his information comes up. There is no reason for you to make that trip, this man is locked up."

"Everybody keeps telling me that, but I need to see it for myself. And please don't ask me to explain to you what's going on. I'll pay you whatever you want. Just give me the proper credentials I'll need to get in that prison."

Ricky didn't push any further. He started doing whatever it is he does and I went to sit down. While I waited, I checked my voicemail to see if Supreme left me a message with any updates about Aaliyah. When I came to the final message I wanted to throw my cell against the wall, because throughout all Supreme's rants, none of them gave me hope that the police were any closer to bringing my daughter home.

I put my head down, wondering if I was losing my mind. What if everyone was right and Mike was sitting pretty in his jail cell with no access to me or my daughter? Maybe I so desperately wanted to believe it was Mike so I could put a face and name to the monster who stole my child, because not knowing anything at all seemed like a worse realization to bear.

"This is crazy. I need to get my ass back on a plane and go home to my husband," I mumbled out loud. Just when I was about to tell Ricky to forget it and that I was stopping this wild goose chase before going any further, he announced he was done.

"You're finished already?" I looked down at my watch and I'd been waiting for over an hour, although it didn't feel like that long.

"Young lady, I'm a pro at this. All I need you to do is go stand over there so I can take your picture." As he snapped my picture, Ricky explained how it would work. "I've programmed all your information into the correctional facility database, so if they type your name and ID number in, your photo and job title will come up."

"US District Attorney's office? That's who you have me working for?"

"As I explained, they run a tight ship. That prison is especially prone to violence. A few guards have been killed in the last couple of years by the prisoners. The inmates are restless and ruthless. Being cautious is imperative, so it makes our options limited. His attorney of record is a man. You're not on his visitation list, and honestly, being from the District Attorney's office is about the only way you're going to get anywhere near a prisoner without raising suspicion. But to be extra careful, take this."

"What is it?"

"It's the certified letter that the prisons rarely require

when you need to speak with an inmate without prior notice, depending on how anal the person working that shift wants to be. They may be in a good mood and verifying your ID information is sufficient, or they could be pissed at the fucking world and want to stick it to you. You never know, that's why it's better to be prepared. Here is your New York driver's license in case they want two forms of ID."

"This shit is no joke. You got this whole covert operation on lock. I thought only the feds were able to get all into a person's private business."

"This country doesn't have any privacy. They're always preaching about protecting yourself from identity fraud, but it's just another way for the corporate snakes to make money off of apprehension. With the right resources you can own another person's life and they'd be clueless until the walls come tumbling down. But the less you know, the better. All you need to do is prepare for your prison visit tomorrow."

"If I'm wrong and Mike is still locked up, I hope when we come face-to-face he doesn't blow my cover."

"More than likely he'll try, but remember, you have clearance, your driver's license and ID will check out as being legitimate, and he's the one locked up. They're used to prisoners showing out, so keep your cool and your only objective should be to get the hell out of there. Within thirty-six hours this identity will be completely wiped out of the system, so as long as you get out they won't be able to trace it back to you."

"So I'm straight?"

"I guarantee with what I've given you, you won't have any problem getting in. Just remember, no matter what happens, remain cool under pressure."

Remaining cool under pressure was my specialty, but I had to admit that stepping into uncharted territory had me shook. "I appreciate the advice."

"I didn't tell you anything that you don't already know. I've been in this game long enough to spot a soldier. You may be young, but your eyes carry years of wisdom. If I had to put my money on it, I would say you're a warrior."

Ricky was on point with his assessment. I was a warrior. I just carried all my battle scars on the inside. Unfortunately, the stakes were so high that I couldn't afford to be anything less than stellar with my performance tomorrow.

"How much do I owe you?"

"Five g's.

I pulled the money out of my purse and handed it to Ricky. "You going to count it?"

"Nope, I'm good at weighing money by how it feels in the palm of my hand."

"Whatever works for you." I placed the envelope with my ID, driver's license and certified letter inside of my purse. "One more thing. Can you print out a copy of all the documentation the correctional facility has on file for Mike?"

"Not a problem." After Ricky handed me the papers, I followed him back to the front and he deactivated the alarm to let me out. "It was a pleasure doing business with you."

"I feel the same, especially if it works and all goes smoothly."

"It will. You're fully loaded with all the ammunition you need. You have my number; don't falter about using it if you need me." Ricky gave me one of his charming smiles as he watched me get in my car. I gave him a slight wave as I drove off.

Something about him reminded me of Boogie. Before Boogie was murdered right in front of my eyes by his own nephew, he was the only person I looked up to as a mentor. He knew the ins and outs of the game and schooled me on it, especially when it came to gaming men. But like so many fallen soldiers, the game eventually beat him. I hoped that wouldn't happen to Ricky, because he was full of knowledge that would be priceless in the right person's hands.

That evening after checking into my hotel room, I took a long hot shower, mentally preparing myself for all of the "what ifs" that could await me during my prison visit. When I got in bed I was tempted to call Supreme, but I knew that small percentage of reluctance I had about going through with my plan could easily grow much bigger after speaking with him. With a few carefully selected words he might convince me to come home and abandon my mission. So instead, I pulled out the confidential information from Mike's personal file and read it thoroughly before falling asleep.

WELCOME TO THE JUNGLE

The non-stop blaring sound coming from the alarm woke me up at three o'clock in the morning. I had a five-hour ride ahead of me and I wanted to be one of the first visitors there.

After washing my face and brushing my teeth, I slipped on the Dolce & Gabbana amaretto and white tweed suit I brought with me to wear for this monumental occasion. I discarded my standard designer ghetto fabulous attire and opted for a classic 3-button jacket paired with a below-the-knee flip flared hemmed skirt, and brown suede Fendi peep-toe pumps. It had the perfect combination of elite sophistication and New York City career woman flare. I brushed my below-the-shoulder wavy hair up into a tight bun. I applied one thin coat of foundation powder, black massacre and clear lip gloss to give a polished appearance. To add one last professional touch, I put on some non-prescription reading glasses, grabbed my briefcase and bounced.

I put the pedal to the metal, pushing it on the highway. My fucking nerves had me so antsy that I felt that I had been driving on Northway 1-87 for days instead of hours. My breaking point subsided when I noticed the exit I needed to take, 38N. Not long after, I was in Dannemora's main business district where the walls of the prison go right up to the streets. I inhaled deeply, counted to three, and then eased up to the first entrance to the prison.

"I need to see your driver's license." The six-three guard was enclosed in a protected armored box that had bars over the square window, and two additional armed guards were posted on either side. The whole setup was intimidating, especially for someone who was trying to bootleg their way in. The guard slid out a metal tray for me to place my license in. My heart was thumping and I tapped my nails on the steering wheel, praying my shit would clear. "I'm not going to be able to let you through. I'll need for you to turn your car around and leave the premises," he said with no further explanation.

"I'm scheduled to meet with a prisoner this morning, so what is the problem?" I kept my tone respectful but with a touch of authority as if I was confident in what I was saying and he was the one making a mistake.

"Your name is not on any list that I have, and I spoke with the guard inside the prison and you're not on their list either. So I need for you to leave now, or you'll be arrested."

I had reached that crossroad where I could put a halt to my undertaking, or push the envelope and go full steam ahead, risking having my cover blown wide open.

Knowing I wouldn't be able to have a decent night's sleep ever again until I stared at Mike's face behind bars, I chose the latter. "I'm from the US Attorney's office and I've been given clearance to see one of your prisoners this morning. So I won't be going anywhere. Do I need to have the head of my department to place a phone call to your boss?" I asked, flipping open my phone as if I was about to dial the number.

"You should've said that instead of handing me your driver's license."

"If I'm not mistaken, sir, that's what you requested from me," I answered, putting on my most proficient white girl voice.

"I need to see your ID."

I placed it in that same metal tray.

"And your paperwork," he added.

I seized the certified letter from the envelope since that was the only paperwork Ricky gave me. I watched as the hard-nosed brotha scrutinized my shit as if he wasn't another low-on-the-totem-pole worker but instead owned the prison, and would lose millions of dollars he invested if I was able to make it through those gates.

After another few minutes of waiting in silence, I was ready to snatch him out of his box and run him over several times with my rental truck. Noticing the metal tray slide back out with my ID and document, I snapped out of my illusions of torturing the watchdog. He remained on mute and I didn't know I had been cleared until the gate lifted, allowing me to drive through. I quickly snatched up my shit and put my foot on the gas before he wanted to get extra and grill me further.

I parked the SUV and sat for a second with the key in the ignition. "This is it," I said, gazing at myself in the mirror. As I adjusted my reading glasses, I noticed the mammoth wedding ring on my finger and took it off. The last thing I need is additional attention put on myself and sporting a rock of this size will for sure bring it.

It was now or never, so I grabbed my belongings, and when my Fendi pumps hit the concrete I became Angela Connor from the US District Attorney's office. I had to go through two more security checks before finally making it through the cold dreadful hall of the prison. Finally thinking I was home free, I had to deal with one last gatekeeper.

"Hello, I'm Angela Connor here to see prisoner 18699-052." It bugged me out that out on the streets hustlers had a million and one different aliases but in jail that shit didn't mean anything, because in these walls they were nothing but a fucking number.

"I need to see your identification," the hefty, light-skinned woman said tight-lipped. "I also need to check you for contraband."

"I've already been checked twice."

"Now you can make that three times."

"I'm from the US Attorney's office. Do you really think I'm going to smuggle illegal goods in here for a prisoner?" I was getting so caught up in my charade that I was starting to believe I really was that bitch with the official job title.

"Miss, you have no idea how many seemingly intelligent

women walk into this prison with all intent to uphold the law but fall for the bullshit one of these inmates run on them, and end up leaving as a criminal themselves."

"Point made."

After checking for contraband, she then patted me down, although I had already gone through a metal detector before getting this far. "You can go straight ahead."

I followed the direction she pointed in. Then I heard a buzzing sound and the heavy steel door opened. I jumped when it clanged shut behind me.

As I trailed behind two guards, I tried to get my thoughts in order. We entered a closed off space and the chilly white walls reminded me of the interrogation room the cops drilled me in after Jalen Montgomery, the basketball player I briefly dated, had been beaten so badly that he ended up in intensive care. They were convinced I had something to do with it, but Mike later informed me he was responsible for the pointless bloodshed—another crime Mike was never held accountable for. That beatdown caused Jalen to miss the entire remaining season, and to this day sports critics say his once-coveted jump shot has never been the same since the incident.

I sat in the chair facing the door waiting for the guards to bring Mike down. Anger began brewing inside of me as I reminisced over all the havoc he had caused. I pulled out a folder filled with meaningless papers and a notepad so it would appear as if I was handling my business. I flipped my pen on the hard-topped table, no longer filled with the fear of being exposed. All that remained floating inside of me was hate for Mike.

I could hear movement coming from the hallway, and from the positioning of my chair I could see two guards on both sides of a man who looked exactly like Mike. *He is locked up! He couldn't have kidnapped Aaliyah. Then who did? Why didn't I listen to Supreme?* I thought. As the questions were darting around in my head, the men were getting closer. I put my head down and began writing any fucking thing on my notepad so Mike wouldn't instantly recognize me.

"The prisoner is here," the guard announced.

I kept my head down, ogling the shackles around his legs, and I slowly worked my way up his gray two-piece apparel to his shackled wrists.

"Is this really necessary?" he said, lifting up his shackled wrists. "I'm cooperating; I ain't give ya no problems on the way here."

The guards eyed me as to see if I had an objection, and my silence let them know that I didn't. Knowing they were eyeing him like a hawk with fully loaded clips, I felt safe.

When the prisoner sat down in the chair across from me, I had to admit the resemblance was uncanny, but my gut instinct was right. The man sitting in front of me wasn't Pretty Boy Mike, but a damn good imposter. He even bore a replica tattoo on the inside of his left wrist of a dagger with a teardrop on each side.

"How are you this morning?" My voice was subdued because I was digging around in my brain on what to do next. My dumb ass hadn't even prepared for this possibility, and I had to find a way to expose the truth without blowing my cover.

"Better than I been in a long time… now that you're here. Damn, you sexy as hell, even with that uptight do you got going on. You the type of woman the big boys got handling jailhouse business now? You can come visit me anytime." He licked his lips at me as if I was about to drop my panties for him. It was crystal clear why the last watchdog felt the need to school me, but I couldn't believe women would be falling for this lame game he was kicking. They had to be straight knuckleheads. I opened my folder pretending to be reading over documents.

"Your name is Michael Owens, correct?"

"That's right." He leaned back in the chair, oozing with haughtiness, and I couldn't blame him. On paper he was a dead ringer for Mike. They shared the same height, build, complexion and hair texture. With there being almost three thousand inmates, no one would think otherwise. I was dying to know how in the hell Mike orchestrated this bullshit and who helped him. "So what can I help you with…" The imposter leaned over and grabbed my lapel to read my tag, "Ms. Angela Connors?"

"Sit back. There is no touching," the guard reminded the arrogant sonofabitch.

"What's so funny?" he asked as I let out a slight chuckle.

Unbeknownst to him, the bright idea I needed in order to change the tides had disclosed itself. "Guard, I believe we have a problem," I said in my most concerned voice.

"Man, we ain't got no problem. If the flirting is making you uncomfortable I'll stop," the imposter said as if doing me a favor.

I locked eyes with the Mike wannabe and paused before speaking. "You wish that was the only problem you had."

He sat up straight in the chair as if something clicked in his head telling him he was fucked.

"What is the problem?" the guard asked, glancing over at the prisoner with a look that said he was yearning to have an excuse to bust his ass.

There has obviously been some sort of security breach, because this man is not Mike Owens."

"Bitch, shut the fuck up! You don't know what the hell you talking about," he barked, standing up from his chair. All that sugary, fake-ass charm he was delivering was gone. "I'm ready to go back to my cell. This broad crazy."

"Have a seat," the guard ordered.

He sat back down with reluctance and folded his hands on top of the table. He struggled to regain his composure, but he was breathing so hard his muscles were flexing through his jailhouse attire. The dagger from his wrist was now coming through his eyes as he fixated on my face, attempting to freeze my words out of fear. Of course, the pathetic thing had no idea he wasn't dealing with a welterweight. "This some bullshit," he mumbled, only further annoying the guard.

"This is Michael Owens. Do you have any proof to suggest otherwise?" The guard lifted his eyebrow, waiting to hear my answer.

"Nah, this troublemaker ain't got no proof. Shit, look at my wrist. That's a Mike Owens' tattoo. Don't nobody have this but me," he argued, extending out his arm for everyone to see.

"You're absolutely right, that is a Mike Owens' tattoo that you had duplicated. But just now, you had to check my badge. The real Mike Owens would have recognized me from past meetings. I'm also willing to bet that no matter how much you were compensated for this sham, you weren't willing to get the five-inch scar that decorates the upper right side of the real Mr. Owens' back," I taunted as he felt the painful squeeze I had on his balls.

I turned my attention back to the guards. "I'm sure if you check Mr. Owens' records you will see that was one of the distinguishable marks listed in his report." I cracked a smile as I witnessed the color drain from the imposter's face. There was no way for them to prove that Mike hadn't met with a US Attorney named Angela Connors, and luckily, Ricky had given me a copy of Mike's profile. If I hadn't read through the information last night, I would've never known how to back up my story.

"I'm going to need you to turn around and lift up your shirt," the guard stated.

But instead of complying, the fraudulent Michael Owens jumped over the table and clutched his hands around my throat. "You trifling cunt!" he roared, spitting the words in my face.

I gasped for air as he chocked the life out of me. I could see the guards using all their strength to wrestle the maniac off of me, but his grip was cemented around my neck. My vision began to blur as my lungs fought for air. To make matters worse, the fool started banging my head against the cement floor. *Why the fuck did I let them take those shackles of his wrists?* was all I could think. I heard a few more guards run in, and it took all of their manpower to get him off of me.

"I shoulda ripped off your head! That's what snitching-ass bitches deserve!" he continued as the guards dragged him out.

"We need to get you to the infirmary." One of the other guards lifted me up and sat me down on the chair.

"No, I'm fine, just hand me that water." *That mother-fucker is as crazy as Mike*, I thought, feeling a migraine about to sneak up on me.

"Miss, you need to be checked out."

"Listen, I'm fine. When I leave here, I'll have my own doctor check me out. Your only priority right now should be alerting the police that one of your inmates has escaped."

"We're already moving on it. If you hadn't brought this to our attention, there is no telling how long they could've gotten away with it. We appreciate the tip."

"I was only doing my job, which I better get back to."

"We need for you to wait. We have to fill out a report, and the watch commander might want to speak with you."

"Of course I want to help in any way that I can, but I'm already running late and I have to be going. I will call you when I get back to my office and you can fax me over whatever paperwork I need to fill out. The commander can also call my office if they have any further questions," I said, babbling off at the mouth and gathering my belongings at the same time. Knowing every second I was in the prison I risked being discovered as an imposter made me want to hop, skip and jump out this motherfucker, but I kept telling myself to remain cool.

When I finally did exit from the confinement of gray concrete walls, I couldn't put my key in the ignition fast enough to make a getaway.

When I made it back to the hotel, before heading up to my room I had stopped at the store in the lobby and purchased some Excedrin Migraine medicine. My headache was kicking my ass the entire five-hour drive, but paranoia wouldn't allow me to stop until I reached my destination. Between my concern of someone at the prison tracking me down, and now knowing for a fact that Mike was loose on the streets, I was triple checking over my shoulder.

I checked my phone messages and Supreme was steady cursing me out on each of his messages, but the police had no leads on Aaliyah. That wasn't surprising since they had never put Mike in the mix. I prayed that soon all the news outlets would announce that he'd escaped from prison so the LAPD would get on their job.

I wanted to call Supreme and the detective to share what I learned, but then how I got the information would cause me serious repercussions. What I did was illegal, and although I had no qualms about breaking the law, getting caught was never an option. With Aaliyah being in the hands of a sociopath like Mike, I couldn't afford to be locked up not even for a day. I had to keep the faith and believe that soon the Clinton Correctional Facility would get their story straight about how they allowed that shit to go down at their prison and make the fucking information public. But all they were probably stressing was damage control, and that wasn't doing me or Aaliyah any good.

Then it came to me. Sometimes you have to force a motherfucker to crawl out from under the rock they're hiding under.

When I got in my hotel room, I opened up the phone book and found the numbers I was searching for. I picked up my burner and began making calls.

"Hi, I work at the Clinton Correctional Facility in Dannemora, New York," I paused so the person who answered could take the location in. "It's a maximum security prison," I added to someone who sounded like an older white lady on the other end of the phone. I wanted her to start imagining big black treacherous killers running free, possibly in her neighborhood, after I dropped dime on her.

"Hmm, hmm," was all I got as I assumed the perplexed woman wondered where this one-sided conversation was going.

I continued, "Well, one of our most dangerous inmates escaped a few days ago and is thought to be in the New York City area."

"What!" she gasped.

Now that I had her full attention, I continued to wheel her in. "Yes, the prison hasn't made an announcement be-cause they're trying to spin the story, you know, for damage control."

"How dare they!"

"I know, I'm with you. I was concerned about innocent citizens, like you, being in danger, so I felt it was my duty to alert the media since the prison hasn't. But of course I have to remain anonymous because I can't lose my job—I have five kids to support with no husband."

"I totally understand. That prison should be ashamed. What is the name of the escapee?"

"Michael Owens." I could hear her writing the name down on a piece of paper. "He is a thirty-three year old Black male, about six-two and two hundred-twenty pounds."

"You've done the right thing—thank you."

"When are you going to release the information?"

"Immediately. I'll call over to the prison and give them the opportunity to comment on the story, but then I'll be sending it out to all of our affiliates."

When I hung up, I set the lines on fire, calling several other news stations and newspapers. Once I felt I had the news trickling, I rushed packing all my shit, intent on making the seven o'clock flight out of Newark.

I zipped up my last bag and was about to walk out the door when I heard my cell ringing. "It's probably Supreme," I moaned, rummaging though my purse. "Hello?"

"It must feel good to be back home. I've tried to picture it, but I can't see you being happy in Cali. You're a New York girl at heart, always have been and always will be."

A chill went through my spine that Mike knew I was in New York. I wondered if he had already got word about what went down at the prison earlier and he was trying to piece shit together by baiting me, or was it something as simple as his peeps hearing I had been in Brooklyn and they alerted him. I decided to try my own bait trick.

"How does it feel to be out of prison, Mike?"

"I wouldn't know. I'm still here counting down the days when I'll be able to finish what I started with you."

"I'm sure it'll be sooner than you think. But wait, if you're still locked up, why did you tell me you have Aaliyah? In your last phone call you did say you were spending time with my daughter... correct?"

"I lied. I don't have our daughter—yet. You know how much I enjoy playing games with you."

"Excuses, excuses. How convenient. I'll tell you what. Since my mood is in an upswing, I'm willing to give you two choices. But this offer is only good this one time."

"I'm a fair man, enlighten me."

"Your first choice is you can return my daughter unharmed on your way back to prison, or you can return my daughter unharmed and die. It's up to you. You have ten seconds to make up your mind." I began my count from ten. When I reached one, I hung up the phone. I had to muster up all my strength not to plead for Aaliyah's return, but if I was going to win this war with Mike and get my daughter back, conventional tactics wouldn't work. I couldn't let him smell not even an ounce of my horror, or he would use it to make me so crazy I would have no alternative but to check into a mental institution. Mike also believed Aaliyah could be his daughter, and that belief was her saving grace. As psycho as he was, he would never harm a child that had his blood running through her.

I closed my eyes and visualized her safe return. In the same image, Mike was dressed in an all black suit and was being lowered six feet under. We were at his funeral, and every eye was dry, including his own mother's. All the visitors who came to pay their respect showed absolutely no emotion. But once his coffin was placed securely underground, the thousands of people who showed up came alive as they threw dirt over his coffin, determined to bury him into oblivion. What a beautiful image that was, and one I vowed to make come true.

WARNING

When my flight landed at LAX, the moment I got off the plane I was swarmed by the news media. "Mrs. Mills, how are you dealing with the kidnapping of your daughter?"

"Has a ransom been demanded?" Another reporter asked, shoving her mic in my face. I kept walking as the reporters kept tossing one question after another in my face.

"Do you think your daughter is still alive?"

After one bold reporter hit me with that I stopped dead in my tracks, looked straight in the camera he had on me and said, "She better be!" They all seemed confused by my response, but I wasn't. I was sending a warning directly to Mike and whomever he had assisting him.

My comment seemed to make the reporters thirstier. They followed me to my car and trailed me as I drove home. The only thing that kept them from walking with me to my front door and having a seat in my living room was the iron gate at the end of the driveway.

By the time I got home it was after midnight, and I hoped Supreme was sleep because I wasn't in the mood for a confrontation. I opened the door quietly, ready to punch in the code so the security alarm wouldn't go off, but the entire house was lit up as if it were the middle of the afternoon. I dropped my bags and walked towards the living room. I heard intense voices that came to a halt when my presence was felt after I entered the room. Supreme, Clip and Maya all stared at me as if seeing a ghost.

"You finally decided to bring your ass home. Do you know how fuckin' worried I was? How the fuck you not gonna answer yo' fuckin' phone and not return my calls? I been stressing over my daughter and then you got me stressing over you too. You on some bullshit, Precious!" Supreme roared, throwing his glass of Hennessey across the room. When the glass shattered against the wall, all I could think about was the awful stain it would leave.

"Precious, where have you been? Supreme is amp, but we all been worried. You should've called," Maya said, trying to be the voice of reason.

"You think I'm not worried? I'm tryna bring my daughter home, so excuse me if I didn't have time to call and pacify you and my husband."

"I guess you didn't hear," Supreme said in that calm voice he used when he wanted to break your neck but was using restraint.

"Hear what? That everybody now knows that our daughter has been kidnapped?" I shot back. "I thought the detective said he would hold off on letting the media know that we're the parents so it wouldn't turn into a major freaking circus. So much for that!" I said sarcastically. "When I got off the plane damn near every media outlet was waiting for me, and they followed me home. I wish they'd put all that energy into tracking down Aaliyah."

"Off the plane…" Supreme paused as if in disbelief, then continued, "Our daughter is missing and you're taking fuckin' trips?" Supreme's solid frame stood frozen with fists clenched like he was Rubin "Hurricane" Carter ready to get his box on. "But fuck that! We have bigger problems than your disappearing act and the media. Detective Moore called earlier today to inform us that Mike had escaped. He didn't have the details, but a guard at Clinton was alerted of the prison break and now there's a manhunt for him. And, Precious, I don't want to hear it," Supreme said, raising his hand.

"Hear what? That I fuckin' told you so? See, if you'd listened to me maybe the cops could've stopped Mike before he had a chance to break out with Aaliyah. Because they wasted time, who knows where the fuck Mike is?"

"Look, the cops are now on it, but we don't know for a fact that he kidnapped Aaliyah."

"Oh, so now you want to still act like that call I received wasn't from him either? I guess the other one I got today was from a bootleg Mike too."

"Mike called you?" Supreme obviously hadn't told Maya based on the surprise in her voice.

"So wait, you spoke to Mike today but you couldn't talk to me after I left you a fuckin' trillion messages?"

"Supreme, he has our daughter. Are you seriously trying to have one up on whose phone call I accepted?"

"What did he say?" Maya wanted to know.

"In the first phone call he admitted to having Aaliyah, and I heard her crying in the background. When he called earlier he was talking bullshit, acting like he was still locked up. I knew he was lying."

"That nigga is so fucked up in the head. What type of sick fuck would steal a little baby? I can't believe we share the same blood. I'm so sorry, Precious. I hope his foul-ass actions don't come between our relationship."

"As long as you understand that your brother is a dead man, we good. What I want to know is who the fuck is helping him on the outside, because he didn't pull off this shit solo."

I zoomed in on Clip, who hadn't put his two cents in the conversation. "You been dead silent. You don't have any words of encouragement for me, Clip?"

"Umm, I mean, that's fucked up what happened and I pray Aaliyah comes home soon. I hate seeing my boss messed up like this," he said, looking over at Supreme. "I knew Mike was capable of some fucked up shit, but never did I think he'd take shit this far," he added.

"I can't believe this man is destroying my family again," Supreme said as if in his own world and talking to himself. "First, he tried to take my life, then my wife, and now my daughter. This bullshit got to stop."

I needed some alone time with husband, so Maya and Clip had to go. "You two can go home. I need to speak to Supreme."

For a second they didn't move, and then Clip went over to Supreme and patted him on the shoulder, not knowing what to say to console him.

"Precious, be strong. I know you'll get Aaliyah back."

"Thanks, Maya. I'll talk to you tomorrow." When I knew Maya and Clip were gone, I went and sat down next to Supreme. "Mike is not going to destroy our family, because we will get our daughter back. It don't matter how many casualties are left behind in the process."

I didn't realize how heavy a toll my trip to New York had on my body until I woke up and it was the afternoon. Supreme was sitting in the chair watching CNN, and when I heard a reporter mention a prison break I immediately sat up in bed to see if she was talking about Mike:

"...The details from Clinton Correctional Facility are still sketchy. Yesterday, the prison's spokesperson did confirm that one of their inmates, Michael Owens, had escaped. From what we're hearing, they are looking to question a key witness who sources say alerted prison guards of the escape, but haven't been able to do so. The only information being released on this witness is that she is a female. Unconfirmed sources are saying she was Mr. Owens' attorney, and others are saying she worked for the US District Attorneys office, but we can't

substantiate what is fact at this time. We will continue to cover this story and keep you updated on any breaking news..."

They continued to show a picture of Mike for a few seconds until cutting to a commercial.

Supreme shut off the television and slammed the remote down. "Where the fuck can this nigga be?" He stood up, and all he had on was his briefs. His anger had every muscle from his neck to his chest and calves bulging as he paced the room. The imprint of his dick was protruding, and he looked sexy as fuck, but this anger I had towards him made my husband seem like the plague to me.

I took in a deep breath and wondered what I could do next, because staying in the captivity of this house with Supreme would be unbearable. "Was the detective able to trace that call from Mike?" I asked, wanting to redirect my anger.

"Nope, he used one of those anonymous prepaid joints."

"That figures. Do they have any new leads they're following?"

"No, they don't," Supreme cracked with an attitude.

"Why are you acting hostile towards me? Maybe if you spit that same fire to the white man, he would stop bullshitting and find our daughter."

"Because I'm not married to the white man. You lying up in this bed questioning me like you haven't been gone for two days, so yeah, I'm more than hostile."

"You really want to know where the fuck I was? I was

out finding answers. If it wasn't for me, this investigation would be going nowhere. At least the cops know Mike has escaped and he can now be considered a prime suspect. So instead of riffing, you need to be thanking me."

"Thanking you for what? You didn't have nothing to do with that guard at the correctional facility realizing Mike was gone."

"I had everything to do with that. You know the so-called missing witness that the news reporter was talking about? That's me."

Supreme stood dumbfounded, waiting for me to connect the dots.

"I was in New York getting the necessary identification to visit Mike at the prison. When I got there, a look-alike was posing as him. It was me who alerted the guard that he was dealing with an imposter. It was also me who contacted the media letting them know that Mike escaped while Clinton Correctional facility tried to hold off on releasing the information until they could do damage control."

"Why didn't you tell me what you were up to?" Supreme asked as he sat down on the edge of the bed.

"You basically called me delusional when I told you Mike was behind this bullshit. I couldn't waste anymore time trying to convince you of what my gut was screaming out to me. Maybe next time you'll listen to me."

Supreme seemed to be digesting what I said when our silence was broken when my cell began ringing. It was Maya, and I was more than happy with the interruption.

"Hey, Maya."

"I was checking to see if you were coming by Clip's video shoot today with Supreme, because my car's in the shop and I wanted to catch a ride."

"I didn't even know Clip had a video shoot today."

"Fuck, I forgot all about that," Supreme said, hearing my response to Maya. "I got some other shit to handle."

"Sorry, Maya, Supreme's not going."

"I understand, especially with what's going on, but umm…" I could detect the begging about to come out of Maya's mouth. "But, Precious, I really don't want to go by myself. Plus, I don't have a ride."

"Then maybe you should stay home."

"I can't. I want to sneak up on him and see what he's doing. I told you I think he's creeping. He ain't expecting me to come to the video so I might catch him in some shit."

"What does any of that have to do with me?"

"You know you're my only support system. I need you with me."

"You're so fucking selfish. My daughter has been kidnapped. Do you really think I feel like running up on some damn video shoot with a bunch of niggas and video hoes? I think not!"

"You right, I'm way out of pocket right now. I'm sorry, I'll just stay home."

"Yeah, do that." Without a goodbye, I hung up the phone with Maya and got out the bed.

"Did you really have to be so cold towards Maya?" Supreme questioned as I was walking towards the bathroom.

"Excuse me? I think under the circumstances I handled her with kid gloves."

"I'm sure Maya is upset about Aaliyah too, but it doesn't mean she shouldn't go support her man on his video shoot."

"Then why don't you fuckin' take her, since you so concerned?"

"I would, but like I said I forgot. That shit was planned weeks ago and I got some other shit I have to handle here."

"Here, meaning at home?"

"Yeah," he answered, elevating his arms up and being all extra.

"Fine, I'll take her. Anything not to be stuck in this house with you!" I slammed the bathroom door and sat down on the toilet. If I was a smoker, I would've run through a pack of Newport's right now. I dug my nails in my scalp, frustrated by the sight of my own husband. *Maybe getting out the house and spending some time with Maya would take the edge off, because anything was better than here,* I thought as I stripped out of my embroidered flyaway baby-doll nightgown.

Maya was standing in front of her building when I drove up to her condo. She damn near ran to my car so I didn't even need to pull up in a parking space. "Girl, I was so shocked when you called back and said you were coming. I know it must've been hard, but thank you so much."

"Actually, it was pretty easy. I had to get the fuck out that house before me and Supreme killed each other."

"Aaliyah's kidnapping is really straining ya's relationship, huh?"

"Pretty much. I heard a traumatic incident in a marriage can either bring a couple closer or tear them apart. It seems to be doing the latter to us."

"It's making me ill inside that my brother is the cause of all this bullshit. Aaliyah being gone is hurting me too, but I'm trying to keep myself busy so I don't have to think about it every second. Because when I do, I just wanna cry and then I get angry because Mike is the one who's responsible."

"Who you telling? Between the police and the private investigators Supreme has working on it, I be hoping that any minute they'll catch a break. Then I get pissed because they were wasting time looking in every direction but the one I told them to. They say the first twenty-fours are the most essential in a kidnapping. Who knows where Mike is right now with my daughter?"

"I know this ain't gonna make you feel no better, but Aaliyah is going to come home safely, I feel it in the pit of my stomach."

"All I can keep saying is she better, because the world will come to an end if she doesn't."

"You ain't got to tell me. I've seen yo' ass in action. God willing, it won't come to that, but if it does, I'll be right by your side making the world end with you."

"That's what's up!" Maya gave me a pound and I knew she meant that shit. We had been through some battles together, and once she even saved my life, that's how we became tight. She was my soldier. "I apologize for being harsh with you earlier."

"Nah, you were right, I was being selfish. Between

Aaliyah and Clip, I'm bugging out."

"Clip still giving you problems?"

"Girl, you know how that female intuition is, and mine is going berserk."

"Well, you're holding it together well. You giving off major sex appeal like you ought to be playing the leading lady on set."

"Is that a stamp of approval I'm getting from you?"

I nodded my head letting Maya know I was. The slim fitting V-neck, intense blue silk charmeuse top with black lace trim and low-rise ass-hugging black jeans were on point. The outfit highlighted her newly developing assets without screaming "I'm desperate, please stare at me," although any straight nigga would. "You'll definitely catch Clip's attention when you walk in wearing that."

"That's cool, but I'm really trying to catch the attention of whatever hoochie has her eye on my man. You know, send her a message that I'm not one of those ole frumpy chicks. If she tries to fuck with mine, there will be some stiff competition."

"I feel you," I said, pulling into the driveway of the mansion on Marilyn Drive where they were shooting the video. "This crib is ridiculously hot. They giving Clip a serious budget to work with."

"Yeah, they using that director who's done videos for Kanye West, T.I., Ne-Yo, you know, a lot of major hitters."

"Supreme definitely thinks he's gonna blow, so this a good look for him."

"True, but yo, its mad cars out here. Where are you

going to park?"

"I was wondering the same thing. Wait, I'ma squeeze in on the side next to that Porsche truck."

"Be careful, I don't want you fucking up your Bentley. You barely even had this shit for six months."

"You right, I ain't taking no chances. I'll back up and park on the side of the street."

"Do you think we should walk around to the back or use the front door?" Maya asked, anxious to find her man.

"I think we should walk through the front."

The door was unlocked to the European-style house and opened up to a dramatic entry with exquisite designs at every turn. With a marble fireplace and cherry wood finished wood paneled walls, the house was official.

We followed the noise to the back where they were shooting a scene around the Infinity pool. The home was extraordinary, but the view outside resembled the typical ballin' out of control rap video. You had a trickle of other entertainment celebrities stopping through for some airtime, then of course a dozen or so of Clip's so-called friends, and last but most importantly, about fifty pieces of half-naked eye candy.

Maya cut right to it and swooped in on her man and the two buxom vixens that were slithering their curves against him. I grabbed her arm as Maya moved forward. "Chill, the camera is rolling. For now all he's guilty of is playing the role of a rich player. Relax."

Since everybody was cheesing it up for the camera as if it were their starring role, it was easy for Maya and me to find a couple of empty seats. I kept my shades on keeping a low profile, not wanting to be recognized. I was overjoyed when I left my house and only a couple of reporters were out front. They tried to follow me, but I purposely drove crazy so I could lose them. But unlike me, Maya did want to be noticed, and she stayed on the edge of her seat waiting to hear the word "cut". Instead she heard the director say:

"Tina, put your breasts closer against Clip's arm and whisper in his ear being real flirtatious."

"Those chicks are having too much fun with this, and so is Clip."

"I know how you feel, but its part of the game. I remember dating Supreme before we got married, and I hated every pretty or semi-pretty female around him. I was so jealous and I used to love to fight, so I was ready to break a bitch off, but I quickly realized it ain't worth it. Either he was going to be with me or be with them. You can't control where a man puts his dick, only what you're going to do if you ever find out he put it someplace else other than up in you."

"I'll be back," Maya huffed and then jumped up to get her man after she finally heard the word cut. I laughed as she put an extra twist in her walk, determined to make it rain on them hoes. The two females remained by Clip's side as if the camera was still rolling. The giggles and smiles vanished from all three of their faces when Maya rolled up on them. I couldn't hear the words that were being exchanged, but the two vixens did scoot off leaving Clip and Maya to handle their business. Maya seemed a bit hype, and it appeared Clip was doing his best to calm her down.

I observed the two vixens go over to a young woman who was in a chair getting her hair and makeup touched up. I assumed she was the principal. She reminded me of a classier version of Angel Lola Luv without the butt shots but with plenty of ass nevertheless. All I peeped was the vixens' mouths running nonstop as the chick eyed Clip and Maya without blinking. About fifteen minutes later, Maya and Clip ended their conversation with a kiss and she came back over to me.

"You get everything straight?"

"Yeah, we good. Like you said, it's only business. He ain't thinking about them hoochies. But I'm glad I came through and showed my face. The only reason we stopped talking was because he has to go change into a new outfit for the next scene."

"I'm glad you feel better."

"Me too. I told Clip I was going to stay longer, but I made my presence known so I'm ready to bounce."

"You sure? Because we can stay a little while longer if you like."

"I'm good, but thanks for being such a trooper. Wait right here, let me go tell Clip we about to bounce."

"Cool."

Maya was about to walk off when we both heard a cell phone ringing. "Is that you or me?" she asked.

"I think that's you."

Maya reached in her purse and snatched her phone. "Oh, shit, that's my mother. She probably heard about Mike. Precious, will you go tell Clip we leaving so I can take this call?"

"No problem, I'll meet you at the car."

"Thanks," Maya said, walking off.

I turned around to tell Clip bye and he had disappeared. "Excuse me, do you know where Clip is?" I asked one of the people working the set.

"He's over in that bedroom straight ahead."

When I knocked on the bedroom door I thought the man was talking about, no one answered. I tried to open it but it was locked. I walked off thinking I had the wrong room, but stopped in my tracks when I heard the door open. The female who was eyeing Maya during her entire conversation with Clip, who I assumed had the principal role came out the room fixing her lipstick and hair.

"Is Clip in there?"

"Who wants to know?" She stood with her hand pressed against her tiny waistline.

"Trick, move out my way," I said, shoving my shoulder against the side of her body as I entered the room.

"You need to watch yourself!" I heard her scream as the door slammed in her face.

"Precious, what are you doing here?" Clip asked, seeming to be unruffled by my appearance. He continued buttoning up his shirt as if I hadn't caught some groupie coming out this bedroom.

"Maya's mother called so she wanted me to tell you we were bouncing."

"Okay, that's cool. Tell her I'll see her tonight when I get home. How are you and Supreme holding up? I wanted him to come through but I know he ain't up to seeing nobody, which is understandable. I'm keeping

Aaliyah in my prayers."

"I appreciate that, Clip, but why was that chick in this room with the door locked?

"You talking about Destiny?"

"Yeah, unless another chick up in here," I said, scoping the room.

"She had to use the bathroom."

"This the only bathroom in this big-ass house? And why was the door locked?"

"The bathroom was available and I told her she could use it, and I didn't know the door was locked."

"Oh really?"

"Yes, really. I know you and Maya are close, but I promise you no shady shit was going down in here. That's my word."

"At the end of the day, that's all you got so I'm going to take it."

"It's the truth. And please don't say nothing to Maya. She's already feeling insecure I don't want you to spark it up any more."

"You said it was nothing, so I'll leave it at that. But Clip, whatever you do, be clean about your shit."

When I left the room, I caught Destiny eyeballing from a short distance away. I was tempted to go whip her ass, not because I knew for a fact she was fucking around with Maya's man, but just for making me think it. Then I thought about all the eyewitnesses and the lawsuit the trick would slap on me and decided to go the fuck home.

The sunlight that was streaming through the windows when we first arrived was now slowly setting as I walked out the front door. As I walked down the driveway and got closer to the car, I could see Maya leaning on the back of the Bentley, still on the phone. I thought nothing of the dark gray car easing down the street doing less than five miles per hour. "You're still talking to your mother?" I asked, hitting the remote to unlock the door.

"Yeah, I'm about to get off," Maya mouthed as I walked passed her.

That's when I realized the dark gray car had turned around and was deliberately coming back in our direction. I made a mental note of the California license plate number. When it coasted to a stop, I knew it was about to be on.

"Maya, get down!" I screamed, pushing her to the ground and sending her phone skyrocketing out of her hand. The rapid succession of bullets pierced my ears as they sprayed my space, busting out windows and leaving shattered glass on the concrete beneath us. I crawled behind the car and grabbed Maya's hand to follow me, as she seemed frozen from shock. For what seemed like an eternity, the sound of gunshots blaring ceased and were replaced by screeching of tires as the car drove off. Maya and I remained on the ground for a few more minutes to make sure the imminent danger had vanished.

"What the fuck was that about?" Maya asked, visibly shaken. We both swallowed hard before standing up. "That had to be the scariest shit I've ever experienced in my life. And damn, ain't nobody come outside to see what the hell was going on? Is the music so fuckin' loud that nobody heard this war zone?"

"And a fucking war is exactly what this is," I said,

picking up a bullet ridden pink stuffed animal. "This is the teddy bear Aaliyah had with her when she was kidnapped."

"Are you sure?"

"Yes, you see the bracelet around the wrist? It has a tag with the letter 'A' on it. Supreme got it for Aaliyah the day we brought her home from the hospital." Staying on task, I looked in my purse for a piece of paper and pen, then jotted down the license plate number before I forgot. I sat down on the concrete with glass surrounding me, holding on tightly to Aaliyah's teddy bear. Instead of this attempt on my life leaving me with a shroud of fear, it flooded me with unimaginable strength.

A TASTE OF HOPE

By the time the police finished getting me and Maya's statements, I was exhausted. They continued to ask us the same questions over and over again as if we would change our story—to what, I had no clue. At this point I was tired of the damn po-po. With each passing day they brought no new information to the table or had any leads. I was beginning to believe they were incompetent, and that's why I held back on giving them the license plate number I wrote down. It was the only potential clue I had, and I wasn't going to let the LAPD fuck it up.

"Maya, it's cool if you want to stay at the house with me and Supreme." After mentally recovering from the ambush, I called Supreme to come pick me and Maya up. My Bentley was destroyed in the one-sided gunfight, and I wasn't about to take a stroll in a cop's car.

"I know, but I want to go home, take a bath and get in my own bed. Clip will be home soon too, so I'm good."

"I feel you. But yo, I still can't believe didn't nobody

from the video shoot hear those guns popping."

"What about the neighbors? They didn't hear nothing either?" Supreme asked.

"Every rich motherfucker on that block was either out of town or just not home."

"Precious, did you see the look on Clip's face when I went back to the house and told him what happened? He thought I was gaming him until he came outside and saw how fucked up your car was—I mean is."

"That car ain't nothing but some metal that can be replaced. The most important thing is that neither one of you got hurt."

"You right, Supreme, but I know how much my girl loved that ride. Precious, remember when you called me on Christmas bragging about the new whip Supreme got you?"

"Yep, that seems like yesterday when my life was a freakin' fairytale. It's banoodles how much can change in a few months. Now I'm living in a nightmare," I said solemnly.

"We at my place already," Maya said, shaking me out of the dark place my mind had gone.

"Let me walk you to your door."

"I'm coming too," Supreme volunteered, turning off his Range.

"Dang, I feel mighty important. I get two escorts to my front door," Maya joked.

"I want you to be safe. It's my fault you got caught out there."

"Precious, you can't blame yourself for this craziness."

"The shooter was trying to kill me. If you would've taken a bullet in the process, I couldn't forgive myself."

"Then imagine how fucked up I am knowing my brother is probably responsible for all of this. So please don't blame yourself, because then I'll have to blame myself too," Maya said as we stood in front of her door.

"I get your point. We can finish this later. You go inside and get some rest."

"Maya, hold up for a minute while I go inside and make sure everything is straight." Supreme turned on the lights and did a walkthrough. "The place looks intact."

"I doubt anybody's coming up in my crib, but I appreciate you looking out, Supreme."

"You my peoples."

"Yeah, so if it gets too late and Clip isn't home, call me. I'll have one of the bodyguards come over and bring you to our house," I said.

"Thanks, Precious," Maya said, giving me a hug before going inside.

"Speaking of bodyguards, from now on you're going to have one with you every time you leave the house."

"Supreme, that's somewhat drastic."

"I don't need your opinion because this isn't up for discussion," he said, slamming the car door shut.

Instead of arguing with him, I remained silent the entire ride home. I had other pressing issues, like tracking down that car. I was so pressed that when Supreme pulled the car into the garage, I couldn't even wait for him to turn off the engine before I unlocked my door and ran upstairs to our bedroom. I went straight to my walk-in closet and picked up the Louis Vuitton Sac Chasse luggage I took on my flight to New Jersey. I reached in one of the inside compartments for the burner I purchased in Harlem. I slipped it in the left pocket of my velour hoodie before exiting, only to find my entrance blocked by Supreme.

"Are you going to move out my way?" I asked casually.

"Why were you in such a rush to get upstairs, and what did you get out the closet?"

"Wow, why do I feel like you're interrogating me?"

"Because I am."

"If you must know, on our way home I realized I didn't have on the diamond tennis bracelet you bought me and panicked. I couldn't remember if I had it on before I left home today and lost it while ducking for cover trying to stay alive. But fortunately I found it," I said, pulling it out my right pocket. "I forgot I left it in the luggage I took with me on my trip."

"Why did you put it in your luggage?"

"I took all my jewelry off. Those metal detectors at the airport are so unpredictable, you never know what's going to set them off and I wasn't in the mood for any hassles. Now, are you done with the twenty questions?" I brushed past Supreme, sensing his reluctance to accept my explanation. It was the best I could come up with on a whim. Luckily I remembered putting the bracelet in my pocket after the drive-by because somehow during the commotion I broke the clasp. I ran with the story, and if Supreme didn't believe it, I could honestly care less. All I wanted to do was get out of his face and make my phone call."

"So where are you going now?"

"To the kitchen. I'm starving. I'ma get a few snacks.

Would you like something too?"

"I'm straight. If you need me I'll be in my office. I have to make some calls."

"Okay." I waited for Supreme to leave before digging in my purse for the piece of paper I wrote the license plate number down on. I made a quick stop in the kitchen and grabbed some random goodies just in case Supreme came sniffing around playing eye spy again. For privacy purposes, I opted for the gazebo outside hoping it would keep Supreme off my trail, at least for a little while.

I twisted a strand of my hair around my index finger counting each ring. I took the phone away from my ear and double-checked to make sure I dialed the right number.

"What's good?"

I breathed a sigh of relief when at last I heard a voice on the other end of the phone answer. "Hey, is this phone cool to talk on?" I asked, wanting to be cautious.

"That's why I gave you the number. What's up?"

"Ricky, I need your help. But first, thanks for the other shit. It worked perfectly."

"So I heard. I also heard about your daughter—I'm sorry. I had no idea until they showed a picture of you on television that you were married to Supreme. I knew you looked familiar, but my sister didn't tell me that much about you."

"I asked her not to. Besides, I didn't even tell her that my daughter had been kidnapped."

"So you think that Mike fella you went to see in jail is the guilty party?"

"I don't think, I know. The story is long and complicated, but I don't have the time to discuss it right now. I need to find my daughter and finally I might have a lead."

"I'll do whatever I can. What is it?"

"You have a pen?"

"Always."

"Write this license plate number down. 5JLE290."

"What state is it issued in?"

"California, but I'm sure the plate number is going to come up stolen."

"Why do you say that?"

"Because I got it from the car that was used in a drive-by shooting today, and I'm sure they were wise enough to use some bogus tags. But I'm keeping my fingers crossed that you can come up with something I can use."

"You have reason to be optimistic. Rarely are plates randomly stolen for no reason. Most of the time if it's still being used, the number can be traced back to somebody in the know. What's the model of the car?"

"I don't know the exact year, but it was an old model, four-door dark gray Acura."

"I'll be at my spot shortly and run the information. I should have something for you within the next hour."

"Good, so I'll call you back in an hour." I hung up the phone and went back inside the house to check on Supreme. His office door was closed, but I could hear him having a heated conversation with someone. I put my ear closer to door to get a better listen.

"...Fuck the cost! Just keep that nigga away from my family by any means necessary."

"Does that include making him disappear permanently?" a man asked whose voice I couldn't distinguish.

"Do I really need to define 'by any means necessary' to you?"

"No sir."

"Good, now make it happen. I don't want to discuss this again until you've gotten the job done. Now excuse me, I have some phone calls to make." Supreme dismissed the man, and I made myself ghost by hiding on the side of the wall. The medium-height, husky-framed man had on all black, including his baseball cap. I was unable to get a clear view of his face, but his skin color ran concurrent to the color of his clothes.

As I thought about the conversation I overheard, I assumed Supreme had put a hit out on Mike, which I one hundred percent cosigned on. I just wanted Aaliyah to be back in my arms safely before doing so. Understanding what page Supreme was on made me want to move even faster. His intentions were good, but until we got a break in the case, Mike was the only link to Aaliyah I had.

I eyed my watch and I only had another half hour before it was time to call Ricky back. I used it to take a shower and then mellow out by having a glass of wine in the den. I sat back in the whiskey-colored, aniline dye full-grain leather recliner, pouring my second glass of wine. When I looked up at the clock on the wall, I was fifteen minutes late with my call.

"I was starting to get worried," Ricky said when he answered the phone.

"Sorry about that."

"Don't be, the extra time was helpful."

"So you found something?"

"I did."

"What is it?" The high pitch of my voice divulged my anxiousness.

"The plates but not the car was reported stolen about a month ago. It was registered to a 2007 Yukon Denali. I then ran a check on the newly issued license plates for the Denali, and as expected, both are registered under the same name and address. I then ran every older model dark gray Acura. That took some time—there are a lot of Acura's fitting that description registered in California. I had the system run a check and flag any name or address from the Acura's list that matched the one for the Denali, and I got a hit."

"Who is it?"

"The Denali is registered to a Vernika Chavez, and the Acura was registered a couple of months ago to a Donnell Graham. Two different names, but they share the same address."

"This is good… this is really good."

"It gets better. This is what I found out during that additional fifteen minutes you gave me."

"You have more? What is it?"

"Guess where Donnell Graham just finished doing a seven year bid at?"

"Clinton Correctional Facility," I answered slowly, shaking my head from repulsion. When did he get out?"

"Three months ago. I'm sure he and Mike started coming up with their plan months before that."

"Where does the Vernika chick fit in?"

"Her record came up clean, but my guess is that her hands are as dirty as the rest."

"Wait, when Aaliyah was kidnapped, they said a light-skinned or Hispanic woman was seen leaving with a baby. I bet my life that woman was Vernika."

"What's your next step?"

"I'm about to make a house call."

"I hope you're not going alone. These people are obviously dangerous."

"Who am I going to take—the police, so what they can fuck shit up?"

"I understand if you want to leave them out of it, but at least tell your husband. He'll know how to handle it. Whatever you decide, please be careful. You're not only risking your life, but the life of your daughter."

"Let me get that address." I wrote down the information as my mind created several different scenarios for taking down Vernika and Donnell. Each one seemed risky with me as a solo act. "Thanks again, Ricky. Do you want me to wire or Western Union the money?"

"None of that. Give it to me next time I see you. Hopefully it will be soon, and you'll have your daughter with you. But until then, if you need anything, don't hesitate to call."

"I will."

After hanging up with Ricky, I had two more glasses of wine while mulling over my alternatives. The police were out of the question. I regulated them to the sidelines until the absolute very last minute. At a moment like this, I wished that Nico had never left my life. He would know exactly what move to make and when to make it. But I hadn't seen or heard from him since that time we made love before he bailed out of New York. Even with all the charges dropped against him he hadn't shown his face. It was as if he'd vanished. I promised myself that once I got Aaliyah back and this nightmare was over, my next mission would be to locate Nico.

Right now, I had to figure out a way to bring Supreme on board without him cutting me out the loop. No way would he allow me to play a part in getting Aaliyah back. He would say it was too risky and to let him take care of it. I wanted to be there when he confronted the two people who played an intricate roll in my daughter's kidnapping. I had to find a way to make Supreme comprehend that.

When I got upstairs, Supreme was stepping out of the shower. "Where were you?" he asked, drying himself off.

"I was in the den having a couple glasses of wine, trying to relax, if that's even possible during a time like this."

"No, I don't think it is possible." Supreme got into bed and turned on the television without so much as a glance in my direction.

I wanted to confide in him about what I had learned, but the wall he put up was so thick. There was only one way I knew to break it down. Although I had already taken a shower, Supreme wasn't aware of it. It would be the perfect opportunity to get naked and seduce my husband without being obvious. I dropped my bathrobe and turned on the water, waiting a few minutes before entering the shower. I knew that Supreme could see the reflection of my body through the glass wall that divided the bedroom and bathroom area. The hot water doused over my body. After ten minutes of re-cleaning my body,

I turned off the water and stood in front of the floor-length bathroom mirror. I moisturized my skin with Supreme's favorite body oil, Satisfaction. With ease and precision I massaged every curve, as if pleasuring myself but in reality showcasing for my husband.

Like a snake sneaking upon its prey, I slithered past my husband as if oblivious to his presence. I let my body melt into the silk-sheeted bed, and when I felt Supreme roll over, his view was of my backside silhouette. I could feel his eyes canvassing over every inch of my body, but he refrained from touching and shifted his body away from mine. Defeat crept over me until the tip of his fingers danced through my damp hair. He latched my waves in a tight grasp, exposing the outline of my slender neck and sprinkling it with purposeful kisses.

"Don't say a word, just let me fuck you," he whispered in my ear as he put one finger over my lips.

What started off as a seduction to gain power over my husband so he would be my co-conspirator, turned into untainted lust. He gripped my firm butterscotch mounds and tweaked my hardened nipples causing shivers to ripple through my body. As his tongue traveled down my abdomen making its way to his domain, my sweet juices welcomed each scrupulous stroke. I clenched the silk sheets, wanting to scream out his name, but remembered that he told me not to say a word.

Once he inserted his rock-hard manhood, I had to bite down on his shoulder in an effort to keep my vocals in check. My walls compressed around his hardness with each thrust, sending my wide hips into overdrive. I invited the pleasurable punishment my clitoris endured as his tool propelled deeper inside of me. I buried my face in the masculine scent of Supreme's body when the orgasmic sensation ricocheted through each element, leaving me wilted in his arms. Soon after, Supreme reached the same level of pleasure and released himself in me, sending us both into a sex-induced sleep.

A few hours later I woke up to use the restroom, and to my surprise Supreme was sitting up in bed watching television. "How long have you been up?"

"Not that long. I couldn't sleep."

I went to use the bathroom and decided that maybe now was the right time to have that talk with my husband. I took my time washing my hands so I could decipher the correct approach. "Supreme, we need to talk."

"About what?" His eyes remained fixed on the mounted sixty-inch screen.

"Aaliyah."

"I don't want to talk about Aaliyah," he said with an aching in his voice that I had never heard from him before.

"I know how you feel, it's tearing you up inside, but…"

"You don't know shit, about how I feel!" Supreme yelled, cutting me off. "How am I supposed to be a man if I can't even protect my own damn family? This shit ain't tearing me apart, it's ripped out my fuckin' soul!" he howled pounding his chest with a closed fist. "I want to break down and cry so fuckin' bad, but I know if I start I won't be able to stop, so I refuse to shed a tear. This shit is worse than death, because you're alive and helpless.

So no, I don't want to discuss Aaliyah until I can figure out how to bring her the fuck home."

"Baby, I think I know how."

"What do you mean you think?" Supreme remained even-toned, not willing to show any signs of optimism.

"I took down the license plate number of the car that tried to take me under. I had a guy that I know in New York trace it, and after some thorough investigating, he came up with an address."

"Is it linked to Mike in any way?"

"Yes, the guy, Donnell Graham, just got released three months ago from Clinton Correctional before Mike escaped. And the woman's name is Vernika Chavez. Remember a witness said a light-skinned or Hispanic woman was seen leaving with a baby? Well, Chavez sounds like a Hispanic name to me."

"Why didn't you give this information to the police?"

"Because I know they'll fuck it up."

"Yeah, I'm wit' you. And we can't afford to take that chance. Alright, I'ma get my people on this, but our plan has to be bulletproof. Everything has to be lined up correctly before making a move. This might be our only chance to get Aaliyah back."

"Supreme, I want to be a part of this. Don't ask me to stay in the background. I'll let you handle it your way, but I'm going with you."

"Okay, first thing in the morning I'm getting everybody together to iron this shit out," Supreme said, reaching over to grab his cell off the nightstand.

"Who are you calling?"

"It might take a couple of days to orchestrate this plan correctly, but until then my people will have their eyes glued on that crib, starting tonight."

I told Supreme the address and listened as he gave the person on the other end strict instructions. A tranquil wave went through me, and I knew I'd done the right thing by sharing the information I got from Ricky with Supreme.

He hung up the phone and a gleam I never thought I would see in my husband's face again appeared. "They're on it. We're bringing our daughter home, I can feel it."

"Me too, baby." I wrapped my arms around Supreme, and for the first time since this shit went down my husband held me back. Hope was once again alive for us.

WRECKLESS LOVE

I woke up to the sunlight streaming through the skylights. A smile crept across my face as if a new day was upon us, and it was. I threw an ivory silk, tie-front wrap around my naked body and headed downstairs to find Supreme. I was anxious to find out what time the meeting would start to discuss bum rushing Vernika's and Donnell's house.

When I got to the bottom of the stairs, I was stunned to see a large group of men dressed in all black coming out of Supreme's office and making their way down the hall. "Supreme, what's going on?" My hand was placed on my waist with hip swung out to the side. The smile I woke up with was now gone.

"Go back upstairs. I'll be there in a moment." Supreme continued talking with the men as he escorted them to the front door. Realizing a few of the men were distracted by the sight of me in my barely-there wrap, Supreme gave me an icy stare as if I was supposed to run back upstairs like a five-year old child about to be reprimanded. But I wasn't budging. I waited for Supreme to shake the last hand and close the door before lighting his ass up.

"How the fuck are you going to have a meeting and not include me? I made it clear last night that I wanted to be a part of whatever plan you had to get Aaliyah back. I have to wake up and find the meeting is over."

"Listen, I got the ball rolling early this morning and didn't want to wake you. I was going to give you the play-by-play when you woke up."

"That's fucked up! I try to include you in what I know, but then you turn around and act as though I'm incompetent."

"Yo, you blowing this way out of proportion. I have no problem including you in anything. It was a meeting. Instead of you riffing, let me tell you what we discussed."

"Go 'head," I said, being short with him.

"Two men have been watching the house since last night. They've only seen a man, which I'm assuming is Donnell. They've taken a picture and they're going to compare it to whatever booking mug shot they get a hold of."

"Have they seen Vernika?"

"There's been no sign of Vernika, but the woman and Aaliyah could be staying someplace else. I have another set of men following Donnell wherever he goes. They are going to continue to watch the house and Donnell for the next day or so. If there is still no sign of Aaliyah, then we'll make our move and take him down... see what we can find out."

"That's it?" I asked, unimpressed with the plan.

"What you mean, that's it? Hopefully watching that nigga will lead us to our daughter, but if not, we'll just have to beat it out of him."

"But what if Donnell doesn't talk, or yanking him up gets Mike to flip and run off somewhere else with our daughter? Then what?"

"Precious, then what the fuck do you think we should do?"

"I think we should give it more than a day or so. As long as your people are following Donnell and watching the house, we should be patient. Maybe in a few days Mike will pop up and have Aaliyah. I just don't want to make a move that will trigger suspicion with Mike and he disappears with our daughter."

"I don't either. But I hate to see time go by and them niggas still on the street."

"Yeah, but at least we have an idea where they at, and that means they can always lead us to Aaliyah."

"Alright, we'll give it more than a couple of days, but on day five, whoever we see, they're bringing them in—young, old, crippled, I don't give a fuck. Somebody gon' talk." Supreme said his peace and walked back to his office and closed the door.

I sat on the bottom step, staring up at the crystal chandelier dangling from the ceiling. I remembered how scared I would be, because for some reason, Aaliyah would love to crawl across the foyer and sit right under the chandelier. She would look up as if hypnotized by the crystals. I knew it was securely fastened to the ceiling, but the idea of the chandelier crashing down would make me cringe. My mind became so preoccupied with it that I forbade Anna to allow Aaliyah to crawl in that area. Those were the types of illogical concerns I had for my daughter, never thinking there was a much more dangerous threat awaiting her outside those front doors.

I snapped out of my daydreaming when I saw Anna walk into the living room. Since I tried to choke her to death, we had only seen each other briefly. I don't know if she was purposely trying to stay the fuck out my way, or if I had been so busy we hadn't crossed paths, but now that she was in my face, it was a perfect opportunity to iron shit out. "Anna, I need to speak with you."

Anna stopped her dusting and slowly dragged her legs towards me as if apprehensive that I would try to finish what I started the other night. "Yes, Mrs. Mills."

"Listen, Anna, I want to apologize for the other night. I was understandably pissed."

"Of course. I still feel guilty about poor little Aaliyah."

"See, that's the thing. I feel you're guilty too."

Anna's face frowned up. "I didn't have anything to do with what happened to Aaliyah...I swear."

"And you know what, you probably didn't. But since my daughter was in your care when she was kidnapped, I look at you in disgust. And if you're as innocent as you claim to be, I'm sorry for my hostile attitude towards you, but until I know for sure, my feelings for you aren't going to change."

"So what are you saying, Mrs. Mills? Are you firing me?"

"Basically, I want you to pack up your shit and leave."

"But this is my home. I left my family to come live here with you."

"Actually this is *my* home, and I was letting you live here. I'm more than willing to financially compensate you for sending you back to your family, but I can't stomach seeing your face one more day."

"Mrs. Mills, I'm sorry you feel this way about me. But I forgive you for your hurtful words. I know you're saying this out of pain for losing Aaliyah. One day you'll see I'm innocent and that I love Aaliyah, and would never do anything to hurt her or your family."

Ring...ring...ring...

"Saved by the bell!" I said with contempt. "I have to answer that. So please pack up your things and I'll have the driver take you to the airport." I wanted Anna out of my house and there wasn't anything else to discuss as far as I was concerned. I went to answer the phone, putting her out of my head. "Hello."

"Why aren't you answering your cell phone?"

"It's upstairs. Maya, this must be awfully important if you tracking me down on the home phone."

"Yeah, pretty much."

"Is everything okay?"

"No. My car was supposed to be ready this morning, and I've been down here for two hours and the shit still fucked up."

"I told you not to fuck with them Jaguars. Them some bullshit cars. Something stays wrong with those mother-fuckers."

"I remember your words of caution. But that candy apple red shit was looking so pretty sitting on that car lot I begged Clip to get it for me when I got my driver's license. Now I wish I would've listened to you. I be cramming my brain, dense on how a brand new car can always have something wrong with it. But any-who, Clip ain't answering his phone and I'm tired of waiting. Will you come get me?"

"Girl, you need to get a damn car service, or tell the dealership to loan you a vehicle until they get your shit fix."

"They offered me some whack shit, but I rather wait until I get my fly whip back. Come on, Precious, you need to get out the house anyway."

"Says who?"

"Says me. I know you moping around the house thinking about Aaliyah. We can go chill, get something to eat."

"Maya, let me call you back. The doorbell's ringing."

"Are you coming to get me?"

"Yes, crazy. Let me get dressed and I'll swoop you up."

"Alright, call me when you about to pull up so I can come outside."

"Cool, but I got to go. Whoever's at the door 'bout to bang it down." On my way to open the door, I glanced down the hall wondering if Supreme had heard the banging, but his office door was still shut.

"Mrs. Mills, sorry for disturbing you," Detective Moore said as if embarrassed.

I looked down and realized my wrap had come loose and I was one step from having a wardrobe malfunction. I quickly tightened the strap and folded my arms over my braless breasts. "No problem, I just woke up a little while ago and haven't had a chance to get dressed. Come in."

"Is your husband home?" he asked as I closed the front door.

"Yes."

"I wanted to share some new information. I'm sure he would want to hear it also."

"Of course. I'll go get him. Please have a seat." When I got to Supreme's office, his door was locked. I could hear him on the phone, but he was talking so low I couldn't understand what he was saying. "Supreme, Detective Moore is here," I said, knocking on the door.

"I'll be out in a minute."

"Okay." I kept my ear to the door for a few seconds hoping to overhear something but it was useless, so I went back up front to where the detective was sitting. "Supreme will be out in a minute. Do you have some new information about Aaliyah?"

"I think we should wait for you husband."

I was about to offer the detective a drink but he pissed me off with that "wait for your husband" shit, like I was the little lady of the house. I tapped my toe on the marble floor becoming restless for Supreme to bring his ass on. "Supreme!" I hollered, causing Detective Moore to jump out his seat. "I'm sorry, I didn't mean to startle you."

"That's fine. It's was just so quiet, you could hear a pin drop. I wasn't expecting..." his voice faded off.

"Expecting what, for me to holla for my husband? I mean since you're keeping your lips sealed until we're graced with his presence, I really didn't have a choice."

"Mrs. Mills, it's nothing like that."

Before the detective could finish with his lame excuse, Supreme finally popped up. "Detective Moore, I'm assuming you have encouraging news for us?"

Supreme's words sounded more like a matter-of-fact statement than a question.

"Not exactly news," he said with hesitancy.

"No disrespect, but why are you coming to my house if you're not bringing tangible information?"

"I wanted to keep you and your wife abreast of what's going on."

"What, your phone isn't working anymore? Because last I checked my number is good." I knew Supreme was becoming annoyed with how the investigation was going, but his abrupt attitude towards the detective had me on edge.

"I think my husband is a little concerned with how slowly things are going."

Supreme glanced at me with coldness in his eyes as if telling me to shut the fuck up because he can speak for himself.

"I understand. We have all of our manpower on it. There are some potential leads pinpointing Mike Owens' location that is what I wanted to update you about. We also found a match on the gun shells left at the scene of the drive-by shooting yesterday."

"Who is it?"

"The gun was unregistered, but it did have a body on it from an unsolved murder a few years ago in New York. We're working with the officers there hoping that case can shed some light on who was responsible for the attempt on your life."

"So basically, you're no closer to finding my daughter," Supreme interjected.

"I believe we're making progress. Cases like this can take some time. But I believe your daughter is very much alive."

"What do you mean by cases like this?" I asked, fishing to see where he was going with that statement.

"A lot of times when a baby is kidnapped from someone high profile like your husband, it's for a ransom—they're looking for a big payday. Or if they have no idea who your husband is and it was random, maybe it's a disturbed woman who is obsessed with having a baby and can't conceive, so they see an opportunity and steal one. But I don't believe either of those options applies here. This seems personal and well thought out. I agree with you, Mrs. Mills, that Mike Owens is behind the kidnapping, but he has a lot of help. There has been no spotting of your daughter, although I believe she's very much alive."

"Is that all, Detective?" By the tone of Supreme's voice it was clear he was ready to show Detective Moore the exit.

"For now, but I'm optimistic that we'll have some updates soon."

"When you do, let us know."

"I will, and I also hope you'll keep me updated if you find out anything." The detective locked eyes with Supreme as if trying to read what was going on in his mind, but Supreme didn't flinch.

"Of course."

"Thanks, Detective. I appreciate you stopping by with your updates," I said, wanting to add my two cents.

Supreme slammed the door so swiftly that I couldn't catch the detective's reply.

"That motherfucker coming over here telling us shit

we already know, hoping we'll lay our cards on the table. Ain't nobody stupid," Supreme murmured while pouring a glass of Remy Martin X111 cognac. "But we ain't telling them *nada*. We gon' handle this my way," he asserted before taking a shot to the head. To see Supreme drinking liquor this early in the day meant he was seriously vexed.

"I have to pick Maya up from the dealership. After I drop her off maybe we can have lunch."

"No, I have too much business to handle. Go take care of Maya. I'll see you later on." Supreme took another gulp of cognac and headed back to his office. He basically lived in his office all fucking day, and it was driving me insane. With Aaliyah gone and now sending Anna back to New York after firing her ass, this huge house felt vacant. There was security covering the grounds, but they remained on mute unless Supreme needed them to speak.

I rushed upstairs to get dressed, desperate to get out the loneliness of my surroundings. After a quick shower, I threw on a cotton-candy pink velour Juicy Couture jogging suit. I slicked my hair back in a ponytail with a baseball cap. I slipped on some shades and felt incognito.

Since word spread that Supreme's daughter was kidnapped, that's how the headlines read, the press was becoming relentless to get an interview. The one and only statement I gave when I was cornered at the airport wasn't enough. They were begging for a sit-down, but Supreme and I both agreed that we needed to keep this strictly about Aaliyah and not his celebrity. It seemed to be working as the tons of press that were initially staking out our house had dispersed, leaving only sprinkles here and there. That was a relief, but to remain guarded I continued to dress down.

When I got downstairs to retrieve my car keys, I remembered my Bentley was out of commission. I grabbed the keys to my Range but stepped back when I turned around to see one of the bodyguards blocking my path. "Excuse me, but why are you standing in my face?"

"Hello, I'm Devon. I'll be driving you around today. I already have the car out front waiting for you."

"I don't need a driver. Thanks, but no thanks."

"I'm following your husbands' orders."

"Well, now I'm telling you to follow mine. No thanks. Now excuse me."

"I can't do that, Mrs. Mills. I work for Supreme. I have to follow his instructions. If you have a problem you should go speak with him."

"Don't tell me what to do. But since I'm not up to arguing with my husband, you can drive me around today, but don't get too comfortable. This will more than likely be your first and last day transporting me around."

I sat in the back of the Maybach Supreme was normally chauffeured around in. The blinds were down on the windows so no one could see who was in the car. The privacy was totally in affect.

"Where is the first stop?" I heard the driver ask.

"Fifteen-twenty North Wilcox Avenue." I closed my eyes during the smooth ride and had to admit it was rather relaxing. When I was behind the wheel of a car, a hint of road rage was always bubbling inside me. But being a passenger in the backseat gave me an opportunity to let my psyche travel to other places. "How far away are we?"

"About five minutes."

I flipped open my cell and called Maya.

"Where the hell are you at? I thought you would've been here an hour ago," was Maya's greeting when she answered the phone.

"I can always not come."

"Stop playing, Precious. I'm hungry that's all. How far are you?"

"Like five minutes, so come out."

"What you driving?"

"I'm not."

"What you mean."

"I have a driver. We're in a black Maybach."

"Excuse me! Sometimes I forget who you married too."

"So do I. I'll see you in a few."

Sometimes I did forget I was married to Xavier Mills, a.k.a. superstar extraordinaire, Supreme. A few years ago I was struggling, living in the projects ready to sell my body to the richest dope dealer. My biggest aspiration was going from project chick to hood queen. Now I was living on an estate in Beverly Hills, being chauffeured around in a Maybach, and my husband was unbelievably fucking rich and famous. On paper this was every hood queen's dream life, but in reality, it was a fucking nightmare. The husband I never felt worthy of having was slipping through my fingers, and our life together was crumbling more each day. In the past I was always able to concoct a scheme and have shit beating to my drum. Somehow, my mojo got missing and I had to get it back.

"Mrs. Mills, are we picking up this young lady?" he pointed to Maya who was walking towards the car.

"Are you new? Because I thought all the guards new Maya."

"Yes. I started working for your husband last week."

"Oh, well if he keeps you around you'll get used to seeing Maya's face. She's family."

"Girl, I can't wait for Clip to go triple platinum so he can cop one of these," Maya said, getting in the car.

"Where is the next stop, Mrs. Mills?"

"Mrs. Mills," Maya repeated. "Dang, Precious, he speaking to you like you Queen of Sheba," Maya joked.

"Anyway, where do you wanna eat?" I asked, ignoring Maya's foolishness.

"I don't care, any spot with good food."

"Head over to Wilshire Boulevard."

"What's over there?"

"They have this Italian restaurant that I love. The food is off the chain."

"Is that my phone or your phone?" Maya asked, reaching in her purse.

"I think that's me. Hello?"

"I've been missing you. Our last conversation ended so abruptly."

"I was wondering when you would call again. What took so long? Let me guess. Being on the run is keeping you more occupied than you originally anticipated."

"Actually, catching up on the missed time with my daughter is what's keeping me busy. I'm enjoying it though. Who knew being a father could be so rewarding?"

"You're sick."

"Speaking of sick, I thought you'd be recuperating from your brush with death yesterday. From what I was told, that Bentley your husband got you for Christmas is full of bullets. You're lucky none of them had your name on it."

"I knew that hit had your name written all over it. You're such a pussy. You couldn't even handle the job yourself."

"Who is that?" Maya mouthed.

"Your brother," I mouthed back.

"Instead of being sweet with the tongue, you should be thanking me."

"What the hell do I need to thank you for?"

"For letting you live. What, you thought that once again you beat death? No, pretty girl, I was sending you a message."

"And what message is that?"

"That your life is in my hands and I can take you out anytime I like, remember that."

"Fuck you, Mike!"

"I'm looking forward to doing that with you too. Soon, I promise. But until then, our daughter wants to say goodbye." I heard Aaliyah's babbling for less than ten seconds, and then the phone went dead. I held onto it so tightly I thought it would break in my hand.

"Precious, are you alright? What did my brother say?"

"A lot, like I figured. He was the one that ordered that drive-by."

"My own brother was trying to kill me?"

"No, you were at the wrong place at the wrong time. That was strictly for my benefit. He was sending me a message. My thing is, whoever he has working for him has to be someone in me and Supreme's inner circle."

"Why do you say that?"

"Because he mentioned that Supreme got me my Bentley for Christmas. How would he be privy to such private information?"

"Do you have any idea who it could be?"

"I'm not sure. Supreme has a shit-load of people on his payroll. Maya, I'm not up to going out to eat. Do you want to come back to my house?"

"Yeah, I can hang out over there, but can we stop by my place first? I want to get a couple of things. I need to speak to Clip too."

"Sure."

"Let me call the crib and see if he made it home yet." Maya dialed the number, then hung up and dialed another number. "He's not home and he's not answering his cell. Oh well, maybe by the time we get to the house he'll be there."

"Devon, there's been a change of plans. We're going to stop at Maya's place first and then home."

"Not a problem. What's the address?"

Maya waited for me to give Devon her address, but she saw the blank look on my face and spoke up. I remained quiet as he drove to Maya's house. I wanted to find some sort of solace, but not even hearing Aaliyah's voice on the phone brought that. I hated to admit it, but right now Mike was winning.

"Precious, are you coming up with me?"

I had drifted so far off in another world I hadn't realized the car stopped. "No, I'll wait for you in the car."

"Come in with me. It might take me a minute and you can keep me company."

"Okay, I need to go to the restroom anyway. Devon, we shouldn't be that long."

"Take your time, I'll be here waiting."

I shut the door and followed Maya upstairs to her condo.

"Precious, I'm worried about you," Maya said, opening her front door.

"That makes two of us. But we can discuss that after I use the bathroom 'cause I'm 'bout to piss in my pants."

"The one in the hallway is broke so use the one in my bedroom."

"Okay, I'll be right back." I shuffled down the hallway, almost sliding on the hardwood floor desperate to get to the toilet. As I slid up on Maya's bedroom door I heard soft music playing. I figured she must've forgotten to turn it off before she left earlier. I wrapped my hand around the doorknob to open the door and damn near pissed in my jogging suit. I gently closed the door and speed-walked back to Maya.

"Damn, that was fast," Maya said, coming out of the kitchen with a Twinkie and glass of juice.

"Yeah, I was in and out. But we need to bounce, now. I just got a 911 text from Supreme."

"Oh shit, let me grab something from the bedroom and we out."

My natural reflex kicked in and I snatched Maya's

arm so she wouldn't move.

"Precious, I'll only be a second. I promise I won't take long. Let go of my arm."

"I can't do that."

"You're buggin'. What's wrong with you?"

"Maya, I don't know how to tell you this…"

"Tell me what?"

"Let's get in the car and I'll explain everything."

"Okay, the sooner you let me get what I need out my bedroom, the sooner you can tell me what has you acting so weird."

"Is what you want in the bedroom that fuckin' important?"

"What, did you leave the bathroom funky or something? You were only in there for a second it can't stink that bad." Maya freed her arm from my grip and started walking towards her bedroom. I wished that I had magical powers that could freeze her steps, but my mouth would have to suffice.

"Don't go in that bedroom, Maya." She ignored me and kept walking. "If you do, you're probably gonna catch a case!" I yelled out in a last attempt to say enough to pull her back in without revealing the real dirt. But of course with Maya being the feisty chick that she is, my pleas only made her more determined to discover what was hiding behind those doors.

"I'ma kill you!" was the threat I heard from Maya's mouth as I ran down the hall to stop her from wreaking havoc. By the time I reached her, the glass of juice she was holding had shattered on the headboard, just missing the face of Clip and the naked woman lying in bed with him. The woman was the first to get rattled out of her sleep by the crash.

"Clip, get up!" the woman said, pushing him so he could wake up. But he wasn't budging.

They had to be doing some serious fucking. That nigga must've cum so hard because he was damn near in a coma, I thought to myself.

Then Maya stormed over to the bed, and slapped that motherfucker so hard, spit flew out his mouth. Now I knew that would wake his ass up. "How dare you bring this ho up in our crib in our fuckin' bed!"

"I ain't no ho." The chick had the audacity to try and defend herself.

Maya paused for a moment, stared down at Clip then reached over and swung on the chick with a closed fist. All I heard was a loud thump as head, ass and tits hit the floor.

"What the fuck is going on?" Clip mumbled as if struggling to come out of his daze. He looked down at his naked body and seemed shocked that his dick was hanging out for all to inspect.

"Clip, how could you do this to me? You fuck this nasty trick in our bed! You could've least got a room, you disrespectful sonofabitch. I almost got killed yesterday, and all you thinking about is running up in some pussy?"

I moved closer to the bed because I wanted to make sure Maya didn't go too far. She deserved to fuck them both up, but I wanted to avoid a murder charge. As Maya continued to cuss Clip out, I peeped the other woman trying to pull herself up from that smackdown she received courtesy of Maya. She looked strangely familiar, and then it hit me. She was the female coming out of Clip's room at the video shoot yesterday. "This is that conniving heifer, Destiny, who was playing Clip's leading lady in the video yesterday," I said, blowing up his spot mad that he lied in my face when I confronted him about the trick.

"I knew you were fucking her," Maya said, pointing her finger at Destiny while she stood there with her five-foot-six framed video deluxe body on display.

Clip turned toward Destiny as if just realizing she was in the room. "What are you doing here, and why are you naked?"

Her eyes widened at his question. "Don't act like you don't know why I'm here. You wasn't saying that shit an hour ago when you had your dick all up inside me."

"Where the condom at?" Maya barked. She knocked the lamp and papers off the nightstand, opened the drawers, and ripped off the bedspread and sheets. "You fucked this dirty bird raw? How can you be so fuckin' reckless?"

Clip said nothing. The silence made Maya fly into a rage. She jumped on top of the bed and tackled Destiny like a linebacker on the football field. She banged her head against the floor repeatedly, screaming, "You trifling ho, I'ma kill you!" After the fourth head flop, I had had enough.

"Stop, Maya. She ain't worth you going to jail over and neither is Clip."

"Fuck that!" she said, continuing her rampage.

"Girl, if I have to pull you off that trick and we come to blows, this is one fight you will not win. Now get the fuck off of her—now!" I took a deep breath, maintaining my composure. I was being patient because Destiny deserved every lick she got. She saw Maya at the video shoot yesterday and knew that Clip was her man. To bring her stank ass into another woman's bed was straight grimy. Back in the day if I had caught my nigga doing this bullshit, a bitch like me would've been plotting that ho's murder and his, but at this point in my life, this shit was trivial. I couldn't stand around and watch Maya get both of us hemmed up on some nonsense.

Clip finally got his strength together and decided to intervene. "Maya, chill. You 'bout to kill this girl," he said, grabbing Maya's arm. But she swung it off.

"Maya, get the fuck off of her right now before I bust your ass," I stood in my "don't fuck with me" stance. Maya's eyes trailed up my body until meeting my face. My facial expression said it all. She released Destiny's head and stood up.

"Are you okay?" Clip bent down next to Destiny and asked.

"Fuck if she's okay or not! You checking for this broad?"

"Maya, you almost killed homegirl. Of course I want to make sure she a'ight. But I ain't fucking with her like that. I don't know how she got in my bed naked."

"Clip, are you for real with this line you're running? I mean come on now, you insulting all three of us with that bullshit," I had to state.

"Precious, I ain't tryna insult nobody. I swear I

don't know how Destiny got in my crib or my bed, and I definitely don't remember fucking her. This shit is fucking bizarre," Clip said, shaking his head.

"Maya, what you gon' do, 'cause I can't stand here and listen to this nonsense anymore."

"I'm leaving."

"Maya, don't leave like this. When you coming back?"

"I ain't, motherfucker! I'm done wit' yo' black ass!" Maya ogled a badly bruised Destiny. "He's all yours. Clip, you'll never feel the inside of my pussy again after running up in that. Fuck both of you." Maya said then spit on the floor between where both were standing.

CONFRONTATION

"I hate that motherfucker! I can't believe he played me like that," Maya belted, slamming the car door before I even had a chance to get out. She had been calling Clip every name in the book from the time we left their condo until coming back to my crib. The curse words flowed and I didn't interrupt once. I remember how heated I was when I found out Nico had cheated on me with that troll, Porscha. It was years ago, but it remained fresh in my mind. It don't matter how many relationships follow, nothing is more painful than when your first love breaks your heart. Everybody handles their pain differently. My revenge was making sure my man got put under the jail cell, so if Maya wanted to bash her man's name, that was harmless to me.

"Mrs. Mills, will you need me anymore today or this evening?" Devon asked as I was getting out.

"I doubt it. But if I do, I'm sure I'll manage without you, thanks." There was something about Devon that I wasn't feeling. He was so damn polite and professional for one, and many would call that a good thing, but it seemed contrived to me. *But maybe those were traits Supreme was looking for in his workers,* I thought to myself as I watched Maya rambling on, waiting for me in front of the double doors.

"Precious, I wanna go back to my place and fuck Clip and his hoochie up. I didn't have a chance to pounce on them long enough," Maya complained as I opened the door.

"Child, please. You did plenty of damage. You knocked Destiny on her ass and probably gave her a concussion, banging her head like that. Then slapped the shit out of Clip, and more importantly, left his ass. That's the best punishment right there."

"I guess, but what if he wife that chick and move her in the crib and shit?"

"That is highly unlikely, but if he do, that shit ain't gon' last no way. Trust, either she will fuck around on him or she'll come home just like you did and find him waxing another ho. This shit don't start nor end with you."

While Maya soaked up what I said as we stood in the foyer, all she could do was scream for the hundredth time, "I hate Clip!"

"What the hell has Clip done now?" Supreme asked as he came down the hall.

"Don't get her started," I said, shaking my head.

"No, let me start. Supreme needs to know how trifling his artist is."

"Forget I asked. That's between you and Clip."

It was too late for Supreme to back out now. Maya

wanted to share her misery with everybody." I came home, and Clip was in bed with that nasty skank from his music video."

"What? Who was it?"

"That trick, Destiny, that's who."

"I can't believe that. Clip wouldn't do no disrespectful shit like that," Supreme said, trying to defend his artist.

"It's true."

"Why, because Maya said so?"

"No, because I was there."

"Supreme, I wouldn't lie about no shit like that anyway. Why would I want to lie on my man's dick?"

"I'm not saying that. You know how women can sometimes exaggerate shit and make something out of nothing. They could've been sitting down on the couch having an innocent conversation, but ya will twist that and say they fucked around and made some babies together."

"Supreme, if I hadn't seen this shit with my own eyes I might ride with you, but it's all true."

"You was a witness?" Supreme's mouth slightly opened showing his surprise

"Yep, I actually peeped it first and tried to get Maya out the apartment so she wouldn't flip out, but obviously that didn't work."

"Damn, I would never think Clip would be so careless. Why would he bring some other broad to your crib and fuck her in your bed? He outta pocket with that. I never pegged Clip with being sloppy."

"I know what you mean, because when I saw Destiny

coming out of his room yesterday at the video set I was straight tripping."

"You caught him with that ho yesterday and didn't tell me?" Maya was twisting her neck and waving her hands like she was ready to slap the shit out of me, but she knew better.

"I didn't technically catch him doing shit. Destiny was coming out of his room and she was fixing herself up looking extra suspect. I confronted Clip about it but, he swore there was nothing shady going down."

"Still, why didn't you tell me?"

"He asked me not to. He said you had been feeling insecure lately and all this would do is get you extra paranoid. I was trying to give him the benefit of the doubt, but unfortunately I was wrong. He played me with a lie and I believed him. I'm sorry, Maya."

"It's not your fault. Obviously don't none of us know him as well as we thought. I feel fucked up in the game. I don't know what I'm going to do now."

"Maya, you can stay with me and Supreme as long as you like, right Supreme?" I caught the grimace on his face, but he knew how close Maya was to me and wouldn't turn her away.

"Of course, you can stay as long as you like."

"I appreciate that. With my brother out of my life and my mother making random appearances, you guys are the only family I got. Thank you both so much." Maya gave me and Supreme a hug. My heart went out to her. She always compared herself to Supreme and me and assumed she and Clip would end up married with child.

Today that dream was shattered in the worst possible way.

"It's all love. I need to speak with Supreme, so get comfortable. Pick out whichever room you want to stay in and I'll be up shortly."

"Okay, thanks again." Supreme and I watched as Maya headed upstairs.

"So, what's up?"

"Mike called me today."

"What did he say?"

"He admitted to setting up that shooting yesterday, but said he wasn't trying to kill me but sending a message."

"What kind of message?"

"That he can take me down anytime he wants. He also put Aaliyah on the phone."

"Yo, I can't wait to kill that nigga," Supreme said, pacing the floor. "Did he say anything else?"

"Yes, something that makes me believe whoever is helping him runs in our circle."

"What the fuck was that?" Supreme stopped in his tracks, raising an eyebrow.

"He knew my Bentley that was shot up was a Christmas gift from you. I didn't want to ask in front of Maya, but do you think Clip could be helping him?"

"It's one thing to be fucking around on your girl, but another to line yourself with the enemy. I know Clip, he would never do no shit like that."

"You didn't think he would be sloppy enough to fuck another female in the crib he shares with Maya, but he did."

Supreme put his hand over his mouth and started

rubbing his chin as if in deep thought. "No, Clip's my man, but beyond that he's making serious bread because of me. He wouldn't jeopardize his career, money and fame for what, to help Mike? I can't see that."

"Remember, he worked for Mike. When the world thought you were dead, Mike was molding Clip to take your spot as the king of this rap game. Maybe the loyalty is still there."

"Clip helping out Mike, that would be some foul shit!" Supreme bawled, unable to control his anger.

"Keep your voice down. You don't want Maya to hear you."

"I already did," she said, standing on top of the stairs. "What Clip did to me was fucked up, but he would never stab Supreme in the back like that. Clip idolizes Supreme."

"I don't want to believe its Clip. But some shit ain't adding up. A few weeks ago you told me that Clip was getting weird phone calls, somebody hanging up when you answered. Then thousands of dollars was being unaccounted for."

"Yeah, and I also said I thought it was because he was cheating on me, and come to find out, he is."

"That's true, but it can also be him holding down the Mike situation."

"Precious, you're making a serious accusation. Nobody can be more pissed at Clip than me, but to help my brother kidnap Aaliyah and escape from jail would make him a monster just like Mike. I can't believe that."

"Supreme, what do you think?" I wanted to know my

husband's thoughts.

"I agree with Maya, but I could be wrong and I'm not taking any chances. I'll have a couple of my men watching his every move. If I find out its true—I put this on my life—I'll kill him with my own hands."

A few days had passed since the whole Clip incident went down, and the household seemed to be in a funk. Maya was moping around missing her boo, and Supreme was frustrated not knowing if Clip was a soldier or a snake. He had decided to put distance between himself and Clip until he could get the answer.

I, on the other hand, was never close to Clip, so if he turned out to be the culprit, then I say torture his ass until he came clean about Mike's whereabouts, then throw him in the ocean. The shit was real simple to me, but I understood that there were emotions running deep on both Maya and Supreme's ends. That's why after I said my peace I decided to fall back, because there was also a chance I could be wrong. The only thing I knew for sure was that Mike had somebody on the inside helping him out, and with Clip's slimy behavior towards Maya, I felt he was capable of anything.

"Maya, I have to go out and get a few things. Do you want to come with me?" Maya was sitting on the bed in one of the guest bedrooms, watching television. She had been in that same position since she got here, and I was hoping to pull her out of her darkness.

"No, I'ma stay in today. I'm tired."

"You've been tired for the last couple of days. Being depressed over Clip ain't gonna help your cause."

"Damn, Precious, I need some time," Ma[
rolling her eyes at me.

"Time to what?"

"To get over what happened to me. I was—make that, I'm in love with Clip. You might be able to get over your man just like that," Maya snapped her fingers, "But I can't. Although I wish I was, I'm not like you. I can't be strong and pretend that my heart isn't broken. I want to move on, but I miss Clip."

"I understand, I really do. Take as much time as you need. I'll stop pushing you. But if you need me while I'm out, hit me on my cell."

"Precious!" I heard Maya call out as I was shutting her door to leave.

"Yeah?"

"Sorry for snapping at you. It isn't your fault that Clip dogged me out for some video chick. I'm hurt, and he hasn't even called me begging to take him back. It's like he don't care that I left."

"He's playing hard, hoping you'll call first. It doesn't mean he don't care."

"Yeah right. Or maybe he been seeing that Destiny girl for a minute and he's happy I'm gone so they can play house." Tears were now trickling down Maya's face and she held on tightly to her pillow. I went and sat down on the bed next to her.

"Don't do this to yourself, Maya. Clip doesn't deserve you, and trust me, its better you get rid of his sorry ass now. Imagine if you had kids with dude and you walked in on some shit like that. You're young, smart and gorgeous; you

.1ave your whole life ahead of you. Fuck Clip. After we bring Aaliyah home, I promise finding his replacement will be next on my agenda."

"You mean that?"

"Yes, I'll find you your very own Supreme."

"But there's only one Supreme."

"True, good point. I'll find you the next best thing."

"Deal," Maya said with a wide smile on her face. It was good to see her with some sort of spark. I was becoming afraid that Clip had erased that for good.

"You sure you don't want to come out with me?"

"Not today. I do need some time, but maybe tomorrow."

"Alright, I'll check up on you when I get back." When I left Maya's room, part of me did hope that Clip was responsible for helping Mike so Supreme could kill him and he'd be out of all of our lives. I hated seeing Maya in so much pain, and I wanted Clip to pay for her suffering.

As I walked down the stairs, I visualized all the different ways Supreme could murder Clip, until those visions were interrupted by seeing Supreme speaking with Devon. "You can pull the car around Precious will be out shortly."

"I'll do that now," Devon responded, heading towards the five car garage.

Supreme made his exit to his office and I was right behind him. "Supreme, I don't need Devon driving me around," I said, closing the door behind me. I sat down on the chair in front of Supreme's desk wanting his full attention.

"How can that come out your mouth with all the shit that's going on right now?" Supreme stated as he stood behind his desk, fumbling through papers.

"Yeah, that's true but…"

"But what? Are you worried Devon ain't qualified? Because I do a thorough background check on all my staff, so you in safe hands."

"It's not that."

"Then what is it?"

"I know shit is hectic, but I'm grown. I don't need a damn chaperone."

"I understand you like to be on your own program, but you not in Brooklyn no more, Precious."

"What you tryna say?"

"I said it. I know you a hood chick. I'm from the hood too, but it's time to leave that behind. We have to be more cautious with how we handle our business. You going out there following your own program can put your life and Aaliyah's in even more jeopardy. You feel me?"

"I do."

"Good. Where's Maya? She ain't going out with you."

"No, the Clip situation still got her fucked up."

"He keeps on calling me. I know he thinks I ain't fucking with him because of Maya."

"So what are you going to do?"

"Wait a few more days and see what my people come up with."

"Any luck so far?"

"Not on Clip, but they might have caught a break with Donnell."

"Really? What is it?"

"I'm waiting for my people to hit me back with the information. But the moment I hear something I'll call you."

"You promise."

"Yes, you got my word on that," Supreme said, giving me an open mouthed kiss. Affection was coming few and far between with my husband lately, but when I got a little taste I ate it up. "Now do what you gotta do and I'll see you later on." Supreme patted me on my ass as I was leaving.

When I got out front, Devon was waiting patiently in the car. Right when my hips got comfortable in the soft leather interior seat, I realized I didn't have my cell phone. Supreme said he would call me if he got any new information about Donnell, and plus, I always felt susceptible without my line of communication. "Devon, I forgot something. I'll be right back." I fidgeted with my keys, annoyed I had left my cell. I tried to remember where I had it last, and Supreme's office popped in my head.

When I entered the house it was eerily quiet. I called out Supreme's name but got no answer. I went to his office and the door was ajar. I peeped my head inside before walking in, but surprisingly he wasn't there. I noticed my cell on top of his desk right in front of the chair I was sitting in. I hurried in to retrieve it, and from the corner of my eye what looked to be a picture captured my attention. Only half of it was showing because it was under a bunch of papers that I assumed Supreme had been rummaging through earlier. I turned my head around to make sure no one was coming before going on the other side of the desk to be nosey.

The paperwork appeared to be an outline of different marketing proposals for some of his label's upcoming projects. It all seemed like unimportant bullshit until I laid eyes on the photos. There were about ten of them, and each contained a picture of the same individual. "Why in the hell does Supreme have all these pictures of Nico?" I asked myself out loud. They were obviously taken by a private investigator, and it had the date and time on each photo. "These were taken yesterday." I couldn't tell the location, but it seemed to be a major city. Some pictures had Nico coming out of a corner store, another him sitting down at a restaurant, a few more with him entering and leaving what might have been an apartment building. My heart dropped as I stared at the recent photos of Nico. His whereabouts were heavy on my mind, and here he was. Knowing this wasn't the time to start reminiscing, I put everything back where I found it, grabbed my phone and left out the house.

"Did you get what you needed?" Devon asked when I got back in the car.

"Yes, you can go."

"What's the first stop?"

"Head to Beverly Boulevard and drop me off at The Beverly Center."

I was completely puzzled as to why Supreme had photos of Nico, but I knew it added up to trouble. Supreme and I hadn't spoken about Nico in over a year, and to discover he had someone watching him sent my brain into overdrive.

I started delving deep within my memory to recall the last conversation I had with Supreme where Nico was the topic. The only thing I could recall was when I told him that I wasn't going to cooperate with the police on the attempted murder charge against Nico for shooting me. I took it too far for setting him up on a double murder charge, and his retaliation to take out my life made us even. Besides that, I explained that Nico was willing to take a bullet on my behalf when Nina tried to murder me, so now both our slates were clean. Supreme seemed to understand and even cosigned on my decision, but maybe that was a complete sham. Regardless, I had to speak with Nico and at least give him a heads up, but first I had to find him.

"We're here," Devon said, snapping me out of my thoughts as the car rested in front of the mammoth, eight-story behemoth of a building known as The Beverly Center. The shopping mall itself occupies only the upper three stories of the structure, but the lower five levels consisted of restaurants and other bullshit that tourists enjoy. I picked this spot because it was busy and nobody could really track my moves or hear my conversation. I would blend in with the other thousands of motherfuckers.

"I'll call you when I'm on my way out," I said, rushing out, not waiting for Devon to open my door or hear his reply.

I took the wavy Plexiglas tube escalators, which snake up the sides to the rooftop outdoor dining patio. When I sat down I clipped on my Bluetooth and got to dialing.

"What's good?" Ricky answered.

"What up, Ricky? It's me, Precious."

"I was waiting to hear from you. How did everything turn out with that information?"

"My husband's working on it. Hopefully we'll have some news soon, but I'm calling you about something else."

"I'm listening."

"I need you to locate someone for me. His name is Nico Carter."

"Nico... Nico Carter..." Ricky took a pregnant pause. "That's one of Brooklyn's finest."

"No doubt, and I need to find him, like yesterday."

"You don't wish him any harm, do you?" I could hear reluctance in Ricky's voice. "I mean, the way your husband, Supreme is a superstar to the world is what Nico is to Brooklyn. He hasn't walked these streets in a minute, but he's still a legend. I can't be a part of nothing to change that," he stated.

"I would never want you to. That's why I need you to find him for me. Nico and I go way back, and it's imperative that I speak with him."

"I got your word?"

"I don't even make promises, but you got my word. I promise it's nothing but love with Nico and I wish him no harm."

"Then I'm on it."

"Appreciate that, but Ricky, time is of the essence and I don't have any to spare."

"Then let me get off the phone," he said, and the line went dead.

Before I could take off my Bluetooth, my phone was popping again and I pushed the button to answer thinking it was Ricky calling right back.

"Hello?"

"Precious, where you at?"

I immediately recognized Supreme's voice. "At the

Beverly Center. Why, what's up?"

"My people called and they about to make a move. I'm on my way over there."

"I'm on my way too."

"No, I want you to have Devon bring you back home and stay here until I call you."

"Supreme, I want to be there. I told you I don't want to be left out of the loop."

"You are in the loop. I called you didn't I? I could've went and not tell you shit. Now, we agreed to let me handle the situation my way. Come home and I'll call you right after the shit go down, okay?"

"You're right. I'm on my way home now. Call me as soon as you know something."

"I will. I love you."

"I love you too, baby. And Supreme, be careful."

"I will."

I yanked my purse off the table and practically did a speed leap downstairs. Between dodging and weaving through the mall crowd, I called Devon, "Be downstairs—now!" When the automatic doors opened, I couldn't get into the awaiting Bentley quick enough. "I need you to take me..."

"Home," Devon said, cutting me off mid-sentence before I could spit out the address.

"No, I'm not going home."

"That's where I'm taking you. Those are the instructions I received from Supreme."

"When did you talk to him?"

"I spoke to him right before you called telling me you

were on your way downstairs."

I cringed knowing that after Supreme spoke to me he then called Devon because he didn't trust I would listen to him. Well, why not make a believer out of him?

"I don't care what my husband told you. Either take me where I want to go, or I'll find another means of transportation."

"Mrs. Mills, you're putting me in a very uncomfortable position. I work for your husband, and if I don't follow his instructions he'll fire me."

"How about this? I'm getting where I want to go whether you take me or not. If I have to get another ride and anything happens to me, you're getting fired regardless, or maybe something far worse. At least if you take me, you can always tell Supreme I threatened you and left you no choice, but you kept me safe. It's up to you, but you have five seconds to make up your mind because I have to go."

"It's your show," Devon said, making the wise decision to work with me instead of against me. With him deciding to step to my beat, I started believing having him as a driver might turn out to be an asset after all.

"Exactly! Let's go." After giving Devon the address, I felt an adrenaline rush as he headed to our destination. I wanted to get there before Supreme, but I knew that would be impossible. When he called me he was probably already en route.

The less than thirty minute ride had me twisting my hair and fidgeting with my hands until finally I unwrapped a piece of Juicy Fruit and chewed all the sweet sugar taste out. "Are we almost there?" I asked impatiently.

"Yes, but for the record, I understand why Supreme wanted you to go home. This area is not safe."

"Safe is defined by what environment you feel comfortable in. Sweetie, we in the hood and that's where I always feel the safest."

I glanced out of the shade on the back window. When the car came to a stop on Myrrhand and Willowbrook, I saw the Heritage House, an important landmark in the city of Compton. Compton was notorious for gang violence between the Bloods and the Crips.

As the Bentley continued to float down each street, the many pedestrians probably assumed one of the various hip hop stars who used to call this place home was shielded in the over quarter million dollar vehicle, taking a ride down memory lane.

As I quickly studied each passing face, it was funny how most thought Compton was predominately Black, but in actuality Latinos held the largest ethnic group in the city. This was just one of the many things I learned when I attended college for all of one semester. I did take pleasure in gaining knowledge, but I took more pleasure watching Aaliyah blossom.

Because I was trying to "better myself" by taking classes at the university, I missed out on precious moments, and Anna was right there playing mommy. That's how she became so attached to Aaliyah, and when I noticed it getting out of hand I had to shut it down. I dropped out of school and decided I would go back when Aaliyah started preschool. School would always be right there, but you could never rewind the clock and make up for time lost with your child. Over the last few months since quitting school, my bond with Aaliyah had grown so strong. Now Mike had to come rip us apart. No doubt he would pay in blood.

"The house must be straight ahead, because it's off this street. What do you want me to do?" Devon said, pausing at the stop sign.

"Can you see the house from here?"

"No, I would need to drive further down."

"Cross this block and then stop at that corner before going any further." I didn't want Supreme or his people to see us, but I also needed to see what was going on.

I scanned the neighborhood watching for any suspicious activity, and couldn't help but notice the difference between Compton's supposed inner-city hood compared to where I grew up. My hood seemed as if it kept a dark gloomy cloud over it. Trash littered the streets. The building hallways reeked of piss and funk. There was no nature or greenery. Instead our feces-brown brick project buildings were reminiscent of a broken down prison. But in South Los Angeles, the yards were neatly situated on tree-lined streets. The houses looked clean and maintained, but any minute that would all change.

The sun was beginning to set and darkness was quickly upon us, and that's when hell erupted. To my surprise, the moment we crossed over the hell had already begun.

"Stop!" I screamed to Devon, surprised the action was in full affect.

The light yellow house was directly facing the block

in front of us, and from our spot we had a clear view of the action. It was like ten deep surrounding the house dressed in all black, with another three on the front porch. Without so much as a knock, one man kicked the red door down, and all the men swarmed in. A few moments later I saw Supreme, and he had two more men with him. I wondered where they all came from, because I didn't see one car that looked out of place parked anywhere in sight. After a few more minutes, Supreme and his men had vanished inside the house and I was itching to know what was doing down.

"What do you want to do next?" Devon asked as if the answer wasn't obvious.

"I want to sit here and see what the fuck is gonna happen. And don't say another word to me unless I ask you a question." I needed complete silence as I kept my eyes glued to the nondescript yellow house. I wondered if this was where Aaliyah had been since her kidnapping, and if finally Supreme would bring her home. "Who the fuck is that?" I asked out loud, but then quickly found an answer to my own question.

"I have no idea," Devon answered, not realizing I wasn't speaking to him but talking out loud to myself.

Instead of making him hip to it, I stayed focused on the black Denali that was being parked across the street from the house. A Hispanic lady who looked to be in her early twenties stepped out, and I knew it had to be Vernika.

"Yeah, walk up in that crib so Supreme and them can jack yo' stupid ass up too."

But then, homegirl wised up, because when she got

closer to the crib she stopped dead in her tracks. Although the door was closed, either the kick-in it received made it look so fucked up it made her suspicious, or another clue was ringing the alarm in her head, something triggered a change of heart. She swiftly back stepped to her vehicle.

"Fuck that! Block that bitch."

"Excuse me?"

"Motherfucker, you heard me. Block that bitch before she can drive past the corner. Hurry up."

Devon reluctantly drove the car up the block until we came to the street that was off to the right.

"Drive a little further up and stop."

"You want me to stop in the middle of the street?" he asked, sounding surprised.

"Now you get it, Sherlock. Now put this shit in park and we gon' wait this ho out." The blinds in the back were still down so I couldn't see her truck driving forward, but I damn sure heard it when she started blowing the horn. "Is she looking at you?" I asked Devon, who had a clear angle from the front seat.

"Yes, and since I'm good at reading lips she's also cussing me out."

"Good. Put up your finger as if you're telling her to wait a minute." I watched as Devon did as told. And like I figured, she kept blowing her horn until she got so fed up she jumped out of the car, speaking fast in her native tongue. The only word I could decipher was *papi*. Her voice became louder and louder until she walked right up to the car. I snuck a peek out the blind, and she was twisting her neck and waving her arms being real extra with it, still speaking that damn Spanish.

Finally when it dawned on her that the shit she was spitting was getting lost in translation, she opted for English. "You need to move your fuckin' car. You can't block the street like this. Who do you think you are?"

"I'm Precious, bitch!" I said, jumping out the back seat as the door flew open. I caught her so off guard that while she continued to run off at the mouth, I was wrapping her hair around my hand and slamming that ass to the ground. "I know you the trick that kidnapped my daughter for Mike, and yo' foul ass gon' tell me where she's at."

"I ain't telling you shit!" she belted, reaching her claws up and scratching the left underside of my face. Her nails cut so deeply in my skin that she drew blood. The excruciating pain caused a reflex, and I let go of Vernika's hair to press down on the stinging from my face. She used that as an opportunity to get the upper hand and kneed me in the stomach. I hadn't had a straight-up street fight in so long, and this thickly built fool was about to whip my ass if I didn't get my game intact.

Wanting to take full advantage of my distress, she quickly got from under me and stood up and looked to be reaching in her back pocket. I forgot about the pain from my scratches, and lying flat down on the concrete I kicked my right foot straight between her legs and the pointed heel on my shoe penetrated her camel toe. She screamed so loud, I knew I would hear sirens any minute. While she bent over holding her coochie area, I ran up behind her. I put one hand around the back of her neck while firmly gripping her hair with the other, and slammed her against the car.

"Where is my daughter? You ain't nothing but a worthless piece of shit who don't even deserve to live, but if you tell me where my daughter is, I'll let you see another day." By now the tears were flowing out and she sounded like she was about to start hyperventilating. I slammed her head against the window, wanting her to understand that more pain would follow if she didn't cooperate.

"I'll tell you where Mike is and where he has your daughter stashed. Just please let go of my hair and neck before I pass out."

Vernika did seem beat down, so I eased up on my grip slowly to see how she'd react.

"I need to catch my breath."

I completely let go, and she turned to face me, inhaling and exhaling as if defeated. There was a gash on the top of her forehead from when I slammed it against the car, blood was trickling down her face, and there were also traces of blood coming from her vagina area where I kicked the shit out of it. I just knew this chick didn't have any fight left in her, until her eyes locked with mine and she charged at me like a raging bull with hands swinging. As I was backing away from her, my heel stepped on a rock and caused me to trip and fall down. I felt nothing but hips and ass tumbling, pinning me to the ground. I extended my hand out reaching for a rock to knock her on her head, but there would be no need. Her blood-drenched torso flopped on top of me.

"What the fuck happened?" I asked out loud,

struggling to move her dead weight off of me. When my view cleared, I saw Devon standing in front of me with a gun that had a silencer on it in his hand. "Why in the hell did you kill her? I wanted her alive. She has information about my daughter that I need!"

"I saw her on top of you and I thought she was going to kill you. I was trying to protect you. I'm sorry."

"Fuck! Fuck! Fuck!" I said over and over again.

Trying to make the most of a bad situation, I ran to her truck, grabbed a napkin that was on the dashboard and used it while rummaging through her shit trying to find any clue about Aaliyah. There wasn't a trace, so I snatched her purse from the passenger seat, wiped down the driver side door handle and ran back to the Maybach. "Drive! We need to get the fuck outta here." I glared back at Vernika's lifeless body then her truck, hoping I didn't leave any traces of my fingerprints. I stared at the yellow house that Supreme and his men still hadn't come out of. It was as if nobody lived on the dead silent street... or maybe nobody gave a fuck.

TRUTH BE TOLD

When I got home I ran upstairs and locked my bedroom door. I stared up at the skylights trying to figure out how this shit got so fucked up. The stars seemed to be shining extra bright in the dark sky, and I was tempted to make a wish, but little girls from the hood learn early on that it is nothing but a waste of time. I wanted so much more for Aaliyah than I had for myself, but after what happened tonight, hope was leaving my body and hopelessness was taking its place.

I got off the bed and went to the bathroom. Standing in front of the mirror, I rubbed my fingers over the scratches Vernika left on my face. They were battle scars I was willing to take for Aaliyah, but I was still no closer to finding her. I wanted to believe that Supreme had better luck inside that house, but my gut told me it wasn't so. Mike was holding all the cards, and the fact that he believed that Aaliyah was his daughter was the only thing that gave me solace.

I stripped out of my clothes and took a quick shower, hoping that Supreme would be home by the time I got out. He still hadn't called me, so I had no idea what type of moves he was making. I figured Devon had reached out to him, giving the lowdown on what happened to save his own ass. Supreme would be livid that I hadn't gone home from the jump like he requested. All that and a million more things ran through my mind as I dried myself off, gathered my hair on top of my head, threw on a tank top with matching boy shorts and headed downstairs.

To my relief, Supreme was home, apparent by the yelling coming from out of his office. At first I thought someone else was with him, but the door was wide open and all I saw was him screaming on the phone. The harshness from his voice dragged my body closer until his words smacked me in my face. "Aaliyah is my daughter, and not one strand of her hair better be out of place when I get her back, or I will make sure that each time you're on the brink of death, I'll bring you back to life and kill you all over again, you sadistic fuck!" Supreme said, and slammed down the phone.

"Tell me that wasn't Mike," I said softly.

"Yeah it was that motherfucker. He had the balls to call me on my fuckin' office phone taunting me and shit. That sick bastard even said he was Aaliyah's father, and I was mourning for a child that wasn't even mine."

"Why did you have to tell him otherwise?"

"Have you bumped your fuckin' head? 'Cause you got me confused."

"Why couldn't you let him believe Aaliyah is his daughter?"

"You're officially crazy. What, you smokin' crack? You can't possibly be asking me that dumb-ass question with a straight face."

"Are you so fuckin' egotistical that you don't get it? The only reason Aaliyah is still alive is because Mike believes there's a chance she's his daughter."

"Are you telling me that you was spoon feeding this bullshit to that nigga, letting him believe that my daughter was his… is that what you're telling me?" Supreme was stomping towards me with his finger pointed towards my forehead.

"I would do anything to protect my daughter. I didn't have a choice."

"Oh, *your* daughter. I'm so sick of hearing that fuckin' shit come out of your foul ass mouth. She ain't just your daughter, she's my daughter too, right? Right? Or can't you answer that?" Before I could respond, Supreme had his entire hand spread across my neck and he had me pinned up against the mahogany bookcase that lined the wall.

"Supreme, of course Aaliyah is your daughter. I was only trying to protect her." And I was, and now I was trying to protect myself. Supreme knew I was raped by Mike, but I told him I was able to get him off of me before he got off in me. Did Supreme believe me when I said there was only brief penetration, and that it wasn't possible that he emptied his venomous seed in me? I had no idea, but I refused to consider that a baby so sacred to me could be the product of one of Satan's disciples.

But I never told Supreme about the night I shared

with Nico. At the time, I thought he was dead and I felt completely alone. When Supreme came back to me, I decided that what happened between me and Nico needed to stay in the past. Never did I think I would end up pregnant so soon. I prayed that the child I was carrying belonged to my husband, although I was never a hundred percent sure. The only thing I was sure of was that after losing my first child, I wasn't going to have an abortion and kill the second. I loved Supreme with all my heart, but I loved and wanted the baby inside of me even more, so I was willing to roll the dice and take my chances.

"Don't lie to me."

"Baby, don't let Mike do this to us. You know Aaliyah is your daughter... she's our daughter."

Supreme fixated on my eyes as if the truth was buried somewhere deep within. He wrestled to see if there was any hesitation with my response. I mustered up my sincerest gaze, hoping to Jedi-mind-trick my own husband.

"What happened to your face?" he asked, rubbing the scratches, which seemed to snap him out of his outburst.

"It's a long story."

"I have time."

"How about this: If you move your hand from around my throat, I'll tell you what happened."

"I'm sorry, I didn't mean to hurt you." Supreme released me from his grip and placed a gentle kiss on my lips.

"I know, it's all Mike's fault. He has us both losing our cool. I can't believe he had the nerve to call you."

"He probably already got word that we got his man,

Donnell."

"When you say 'got him', does that mean he is dead or alive?"

"He's alive. My people have him stashed up in one of my spots. But he ain't telling us shit. I want the nigga dead, but he's our only link to Mike right now. I wanted the chick, Vernika, because it would've probably been easier to break her, but when we came outside she was dead in the middle of the fuckin' street. We had to haul ass out of there because we could hear the police sirens coming."

"Did you see any indication that Aaliyah had been there?"

"Nope, and we ransacked the joint from top to bottom. But I definitely think that nigga, Donnell knows where the fuck Mike is keeping her. He's riding the shit out hard though. My men beat the shit out of him, but still nothing. I want to know who killed homegirl though. That bullshit can't be no coincidence."

"I guess you haven't spoken to Devon yet?"

"Nah, my cell went dead and I haven't had a chance to call him. Why, did something happen?"

"You know when you asked me about my scratches?"

"Oh, I know that motherfucker ain't responsible for that shit!" Supreme was getting cranked up again, and I had to calm him down before he got out of control.

"Hell no! Vernika did it."

Supreme put his head down and started shaking it from side to side.

"Yo, you so fuckin' hard headed. I told you to go home. You murdered that chick?"

"No. I had Devon take me to the house. I wanted to

see what was going on. We were parked on a side street and I saw Vernika pulling up in her Denali. She must've figured out that something was wrong, because she got out the truck and then turned around and got right back inside. I couldn't let her bounce like that, so I made Devon block her car."

"I can't believe you're telling me this shit. We needed her alive."

"I know. It wasn't my intention for her to end up dead."

"So what the fuck happened?"

"She got out of her truck cursing out Devon, and when she got to the car window I got out and we started fighting. I only wanted to beat information about Aaliyah out of her, but then Devon ended up shooting her."

"Devon killed her? Why?"

"She jumped on top of me and her back was facing his. He thought she was going to use the weapon she had in her back pocket to kill me, so Devon killed her first."

"This bullshit was going on while we were sitting up in that fuckin' house? Why didn't you call me when you saw her car pull up? My men could've handled it."

"It all happened so fast, I didn't have time to think it out. All I knew was that I couldn't let her leave because she was a link to Aaliyah."

"Now that link is dead, and the other link wanna be a soldier and not tell us shit. What a fucked up operation this turned out to be. I'm grateful that Devon saved your life, but I can't believe he murdered that girl. What type of weapon was she packing?"

"I think it was a knife, but honestly I don't know.

When we first started fighting she was reaching in her back pocket for something, but I didn't give her a chance to let me see what it was. Devon probably panicked and decided to shoot to kill. He probably figured you would be pissed at him for even taking me to the house, and if anything happened to me you would have him dealt with. So don't be too hard on him. Honestly, I'm glad he was there."

"He's still going to be dealt with. If he had followed my instructions and brought you home none of this would've went down."

"Supreme, it wasn't his fault. I didn't give him a choice. It was basically either you take me or I'll find another way."

"If it's that difficult for him, then he don't need to be driving you around. I'll find a more suitable duty for him to tend to. Damn, Precious, this shit is out of control." Supreme fell back on the coffee-brown leather couch and put his hands behind his neck.

My eyes darted over to a picture of me, him and Aaliyah that was placed on top of his desk. The smile on his face was in complete contrast to the conquered frown on his face right now. I walked over and sat down next to him on the couch. I put my hand on his upper leg and his body felt so tense. "Baby, I'm sorry I didn't listen to you. I'm sorry for many things. I know things are out of control right now, but we will get our daughter back."

"I want to believe that too, but shit keeps falling apart. Every time I think we're making gain, we end up having to take a leap back."

"I know what you mean. But we have to keep the faith. You know I'm not the one to call on God and be the religious type, but times like this I think it's the only way you can cope. Ms. Duncan, the lady who used to babysit me when I was a little girl, would always say if God takes you to it, He'll take you through it. Back then those words were idle chatter, but at this moment they mean so much more."

"I hear you, Precious," Supreme said, standing up. "But when you're dealing with scum like Pretty Boy Mike, the only way to get through it is with ammunition. The way Ms. Duncan schooled you, my pops spit his knowledge to me, and he said it's better to be judged by twelve then carried by six. This right here comes down to Mike's life, or me and my family's life. I rather be facing time for ending his life than take a chance on it being the other way around."

"I feel you on that and you know I'm down for whatever, but..." I stopped mid-sentence as our conversation came to a halt by a knock on the door.

"Sorry, to interrupt boss, but Clip is here."

"Send him back."

"What is Clip doing here?"

"I told him to come over."

"You found out something? Is he involved?" I stood up ready to jump on Clip when he came swaggering through the door.

"Chill, sit back down and let me handle this."

"Supreme, what's up, my man?" Clip said giving Supreme a handshake. "Precious," he nodded his head shyly, knowing I wasn't fucking with him because of that Destiny shit. He had no clue I was also suspecting he was being a soldier boy for Mike.

"Maintaining," Supreme countered.

"I've been trying to get in touch with you. I was starting to think you had pushed my album back or was dropping me from the label." He tried to joke but you could hear the panic.

"Why would I do that?"

Clip then slanted his eyes in my direction trying to get my vibe, but I gave him no rhythm. "Well, I'm sure you heard about what went down with me and Maya a few days ago. It was a huge misunderstanding, but I know she's close to your family."

"Yeah she is, but so are you."

"I appreciate that, because you like a brother to me."

"You're like a brother to me too, that's why I wanted to include you in on what's going down right now. But of course this has to stay between us."

"No doubt. It won't leave this room."

"I think we might have made some headway with getting Aaliyah back."

"Word? That's what's up! The police got a suspect?"

"Yeah, it's Mike."

"Oh shit, he did take Aaliyah! We all heard he escaped from jail, but I was hoping he didn't go out like that. I can't believe that motherfucker would kidnap a child. Un-fuckin' believable," Clip's voice trailed off. "So, what's the cops' next move?"

"I'm not sitting around waiting on their next move. I'm making my own moves."

"I know that's right. If it was my seed I'd be doing the exact same shit. You need me to help you out in any way?"

"I know you used to do some shit for Mike in the drug game. Did he ever mention a dude by the name of Donnell Graham?"

Clip stood quiet for a few moments as if pondering hard over Supreme's question. "Nope, that name don't sound familiar. Does he go by a nickname?"

"If so, I don't know it."

"Why, what that kid got to do with anything?"

"He's the one that helped Mike break out of jail, and I also believe he assisted with the kidnapping of my daughter."

"Why you think that?"

"'Cause they were locked up together until Donnell got released a few months ago."

"That would make sense. So you got any leads on how to track this Donnell cat down? From what you saying, he seems to be that link you need."

"As a matter of fact, I got my people holding him now."

"Word? You got dude on lock?"

"Yeah, but he ain't cooperating. I was hoping that if you knew anything about him I could use the information against him. You know, like if you knew where his family or kids laid their heads at. You know something to motivate him to start singing about Mike."

"I wish I could help you, but dude's name don't sound familiar."

"You know that apartment I got over there in West Hollywood that I sometimes let artist stay at?"

"Yeah, yeah, yeah, I've been to that spot a few times."

"Well, that's where I got Donnell stashed out. I got a couple of men over there watching him. I'ma keep him on lock for a few more days hoping he'll crack. I know you still got connects in the drug game, so I would appreciate if you could make some calls and see if you can come up with anything on that nigga."

"I'm on it. Whatever you need, you my brother, and anybody that would kidnap a baby belong in a jail cell or six feet under. So if I can help bring that nigga, Mike down, then so be it."

Clip was putting on his best "I'm down for the cause" voice. Looking at that pretty motherfucker made me have a throwback Christopher Williams moment, only an updated new millennium version.

"I thought it was your voice I heard. What are you doing here?" Maya questioned, catching us all off guard as she pushed her way through the door. She stood with her arms crossed, giving Clip the head-to-toe stare down.

"Maya, I came to speak to Supreme, that's all," Clip explained, looking uncomfortable.

"Speak to Supreme about what?"

"That's between me and Supreme, no disrespect."

"I already told Supreme about that foul ass shit you did with Destiny, so you late."

"That's not what I was discussing with him, and if you would pick up the phone and talk to me, you'd know that nothing happened between me and Destiny."

"First of all, you have called me once in the last, what, four or five days? And furthermore, I can't believe you still rolling with that same whack-ass story."

"Look, I'm not about to get into this with you in front of Supreme and Precious. They have real problems," Clip said emphatically. "This shit you beefing about is petty."

"Petty? Would this shit be petty to you if you had came home and found me butt-ass naked in bed with another nigga? Nah, so don't stand there and say this shit is petty. Yo' monkey ass is petty."

"Supreme, Precious, I'm sorry the two of you have to be caught in the middle of this. If I find out anything I'll let you, but, umm, I need to be going." Clip had embarrassed stamped on his face.

"Don't apologize to them, you was just telling Supreme that he was like a brother to you. Well, that's what family do, get in the middle of bullshit."

"It's not a problem, Clip," Supreme said.

"Thanks, but I'll definitely look into that for you. And of course I'm keeping Aaliyah in my prayers."

Maya continued to frown up her face as Clip brushed past her to leave. With her frustration getting the best of her, she turned around to catch up with Clip before he left.

"That was an interesting performance. Now clue me in on what it was about," I said to Supreme. I knew there had to be a reasonable explanation for all that schmoozing he did with Clip.

"I still don't believe Clip is helping Mike, but if I'm wrong, this will prove it once and for all."

"How is that?"

"Mike knows that I have Donnell and he's gonna want to cut him loose. If Clip thinks he knows where

Donnell is, then he'll tell Mike, and of course they'll come looking for him."

"Do you really want to take that chance of them actually being able to get to Donnell?"

"I'm not crazy. I didn't give Clip the right location. If some people run up on that apartment in West Hollywood, they won't find Donnell and I'll know the only person responsible for leaking the information is Clip."

"That's true."

"Not only do I have a lot of money invested in Clip, I also got a lot of love for him. I'm praying that when he said I'm like a brother to him he meant that shit. But I don't have time to waste. I need to know now if he's loyal."

"Hipping him to the Donnell shit was a good look. If he is in cahoots with Mike, then this setup will let us know. But, um, dealing with all this bullshit today has made me tired. I'm calling it a night."

"Yeah, fighting in the street will do that to you."

"Funny. Are you coming up?"

"I have some calls to make. I'll be up when I'm done."

"Okay." I walked over and gave Supreme a kiss goodnight and headed upstairs. I knocked on Maya's bedroom door before going to my room, but she wasn't there. I figured she must be outside having it out with Clip. That's what your first love will have you doing— trying to fix some shit that you know is fucking broke.

When I got to my room, I checked my cell phone and saw that Ricky had called a few times. I hit him right back, anxious to hear what was up.

"You hard to reach," Ricky said, answering his phone.

"Sorry 'bout that. I had a crazy night."

"Well, it's about to get crazier."

"What you mean?"

"I took your word when you said that you didn't want to bring Nico any harm."

"It's the truth. I put that on everything."

"So that means you have no idea nor are you playing any part in what your husband is up to?" There was a long period of silence on the line before Ricky proceeded. "I need you to be straight up with me, Precious, if you want me to continue to help you out."

"Earlier today I did come across some photos of Nico in Supreme's office. It looked as if they were taken by a private investigator. It got me a little worried, like maybe Nico could be in trouble. I wanted to get in touch with him, you know, give him a warning. But then I could've been jumping the gun and making something out of nothing."

"No, your first instinct to think there was trouble is correct. It hasn't spread through the streets because Supreme is doing an excellent job of keeping the information on the low, but a reliable source told me that your husband wants Nico dead."

"What? Why?"

"I was hoping you could tell me."

"Does Nico know?"

"I doubt it. Word is, it was supposed to happen a couple of weeks ago, but when your daughter got kidnapped Supreme put on the brakes, but told his people to keep close tabs on Nico."

"Do you know where Nico is?"

"He's supposed to be in Chicago, but from what I understand he'll be in New York tomorrow."

"For how long?"

"I'm not sure. But I'm hearing that he comes to New York often. It's just that he keeps a real low profile. Only a few people know when he stops through."

"I'll be there tomorrow." The words flowed out my mouth so fast I didn't give myself time to think about how I would make it happen, but I just knew I would. "Is there anyway you can follow Nico so when I get there you can take me right to him?"

"I'm already on it."

"Good, because I'm coming in and flying right back out. Do you know what time he's arriving?"

"They say he's taking a flight from Chicago first thing in the morning, arriving at JFK."

"Alright, so I'll be there early afternoon. I'll call you when I arrive."

"I'll talk to you then."

When I hung up with Ricky, my stomach was doing somersaults. I couldn't believe Supreme was plotting Nico's murder, or why. Was it payback for him shooting me? I was so over that, but maybe Supreme wasn't. Or did Supreme find out that I slept with Nico when I thought he was dead? But I didn't tell anybody about that night. Whatever the reason was, as much as I loved Supreme, I couldn't let him kill Nico—period.

I got back on the phone and made a flight reservation for the first thing smoking in the morning. A six-forty-five a.m. flight was the earliest one available and I took it.

While I thought about the excuse I would give Supreme for having to leave so early in the morning and then not coming back home until the middle of the night, I began on my search through Vernika's purse. She had some tampons, lotion, lipstick and other random bullshit that females keep in their possession. I wasn't coming across anything worth my while. As I was about to go through her wallet, I almost fell off the bed when Supreme caught me off guard, "Hey, baby, you startled me. I thought you were going to be downstairs for a minute making phone calls."

"Me too, but some shit can't be handled on the phone."

"What's wrong?"

"I have to go to the studio. They having some major problems I have to iron out."

"You're going over there now?'

"No because the engineer has another session that he has to wrap up. I'm tired as hell, so I'ma lay down for a couple of hours and get some rest, then head over because I know we won't get done until the sun come up."

While Supreme took off his clothes, I discreetly tossed Vernika's purse under the bed. I doubted seriously that I would find any relevant information in her purse, but I didn't want to share with Supreme until I knew for sure.

"Oh, baby, I was checking my messages and I totally forgot that Ms. Duncan had told me she would be coming to LA tomorrow."

"Who?"

"Ms. Duncan. You remember, the lady I told you about who used to babysit me when I was a little girl. She's basically the only family I have. She put my mother's funeral together for me."

"Oh yeah, I think I do remember you mentioning her a few times. Why is she coming to LA?"

"They're having some huge church seminar here and she's attending. She's very religious. When I told her about Aaliyah, she suggested I join her. It slipped my mind until I listened to her message and she gave me her flight information."

"You're going to the church seminar with her?" Supreme asked, not hiding his surprise.

"I know that's not really my thing, but I think it'll be good for me, you know, with everything going on."

"That's cool. I think you should go. What time do you have to pick her up from the airport? I'll have one of the security men take you and stay with you at the seminar."

"Baby, please don't have me take security."

"What are talking about? You need security."

"I'm going to church, Supreme. I'll be safe there. Plus, Ms. Duncan is older. Having security with us might give the poor woman a heart attack. I promise I'll call you frequently so you'll know I'm safe."

"You better."

"I will, but only if you hold me until I fall asleep," I whispered in his ear

"Oh, I was doing that anyway."

I laid my head on Supreme's chest and wrapped my legs between his legs. My body felt so safe with his muscular arms cradling me. I did love my husband, but I didn't trust him, and I had a feeling that he didn't trust me either.

FIRST LOVE

When I landed at JFK, the first call I made was to my husband. It was noon in LA, and I needed to call him before he even had an opportunity to start worrying about me. The studio situation worked out perfectly for me. When I woke up, Supreme was gone. Since I wasn't taking any luggage, all I had to do was quickly get dressed and get my ass to the airport. Now that I landed in NYC safely, making sure home was straight was first on the agenda.

"Hey, baby, I was just checking in," I said in my most innocent voice possible, which was a stretch since everyone knew there was nothing remotely innocent about me.

"How's everything?"

"Good. Her flight got in really early so I'm beat. But it's wonderful seeing Ms. Duncan. We finished eating a little while ago, and now we're heading to the seminar. How's it going with you?"

"I'm just now getting out the studio. I'm on my way

home to handle a few things, get some sleep, then I have to come back. Dealing with the Aaliyah situation made me cut everybody off, and instead of them motherfuckers holding shit together it's all fucked up. Even Clip's shit ain't right, and that shit was due a minute ago. So much is fucked up, but I have to fix it and be done with it."

"Don't get too stressed."

"I'm past that."

"What time will you be home so I can wait up for you?" I asked, checking his schedule so I could know how much time I was playing with. While playing my position with Supreme on the phone, I was making my way outside to where Ricky was waiting for me. He was in a black Lincoln, and I put my finger over my mouth to let him know to be quiet when I got in the car. I didn't want to give Supreme any reason to get wary about the lines I was kicking.

"As much as I would love to hold you like I did last night, don't wait up for me. You'll be in a deep sleep by the time I get home."

"Damn, I'm missing you already. But I have to go. Ms. Duncan is waiting for me. If you see Maya when you get home, tell her I'll call her later on. I didn't have a chance to talk to her before I left this morning."

"I will. Be safe and make sure you call me later on to let me know you're good."

"Will do. I love you."

"Love you too."

I flipped my phone closed, happy I made it through round one of the check in.

"I see that you're a veteran liar," Ricky said, smiling at me through the rear view mirror.

"You call it lying, I call it survival tactics."

"Point made."

"Tell me you know exactly where Nico is, because I have no time to waste. My flight leaves at eight-fifty-five. That gives me roughly five hours to get this shit done."

"I know you're on a tight schedule and I got you," Ricky reassured me as he exited the airport, taking the left ramp onto the Van Wyck Expressway. "Nico must be awfully special for you to come all this way to speak with him for a couple of hours."

"Are you expecting me to comment on that statement?"

"I was simply making an observation."

"Like I told you, Nico and I have a long history together. He's also my first love."

"Those are pretty hard to shake. I still have a soft spot for my first love."

I couldn't help but laugh thinking about a suave older cat like Ricky pining over his first love. "You're right, but I'm in love with my husband and we're going through enough. I don't need anymore bullshit to add to the plate."

"So why are you interfering in what your husband has planned for Nico? Why not stay out of it and let the cards fall where they may?"

"I owe Nico. He risked his life for me one time."

"He also tried to take it," Ricky reminded me as if I'd forgotten.

"So you heard about that rumor."

158

"I did some research when you asked me to track him down. I heard originally you accused Nico, but then somewhere down the line you recanted your story and the charges were dropped against him. That right there tells me there is a lot of history, but I won't ask you to dig out none of your skeletons."

"As if I would tell. I'll leave it up to you to use your own imagination putting the pieces of that puzzle together. The only thing I will confirm is that if I can keep Nico alive, then I will, even if it means being disloyal to my husband."

For the rest of the drive there was silence between Ricky and me. I didn't know what was on his mind, but mine was on Nico. I hadn't seen him in so long, and I didn't know how much had changed in his life. The last time we saw each other he was on the run, and I was tracking Supreme's killer. Fast forward: and not only do I have a child, but my husband is very much alive and apparently wants Nico dead. The last part I'm having difficulty trying to comprehend.

I glanced out the window and noticed Ricky turning onto Avenue of the Americas. He then pulled up in front of the Tribeca Grand Hotel. I was stunned that we were stopping in Tribeca, which was located in lower Manhattan. "Why are we stopping here, Ricky? What, you dropping some drugs off for some rich white man?" I said like I was joking but was very serious.

"No, this is where Nico is staying."

"Excuse me? Why the fuck would Nico be staying between the sectors of high finance and high fashion?

Although he likes money and clothes, this neighborhood don't reflect Brooklyn or the type of people he would enjoy chilling with." The moment the words left my mouth, the answer became evident. "That's the exact reason he *is* staying here. He doesn't have to worry about seeing nobody from BK. He can make his moves on the low without bringing attention to himself."

"Exactly. From what I understand, every time he comes to New York, this is the only hotel he stays at."

"This place costs a pretty penny. I guess business has picked back up for him."

"No doubt. You know Nico was always a major player. Once he got word that all charges had been dropped against him, the streets were his again. But from what I hear, he keeps his moves a lot more discreet now. After what went down with Ritchie, he doesn't trust anybody. No more partners, He's strictly solo."

Hearing the name Ritchie made all the foul shit that went down flash through my head. That nigga was a straight snake. He had no qualms about fucking me or fucking over Nico, and it wasn't because he had an axe to grind like I did. He was just a weak jealous cat. He couldn't stand the respect that Brooklyn and the surrounding boroughs had for Nico. If that nigga said, "Stand up," then that's what BK was doing. I felt no guilt that I was responsible for Nico snuffing Ritchie out, because if he hadn't, it would've ended up the other way around.

"That's the best way to move. I'm glad Nico is back on the come-up. The more I think about it, it ain't strange that he picked this spot to rest his head at. On our first date he took me to this joint called Butter. The place was sexy, and it was full of white model-type looking motherfuckers. Shit, this nigga the one who hipped me to Rodeo Drive." Those memories brought a smile to my face.

"Nico always moved in style. He's one of the few younger cats in the game I have respect for. He's a good dude, real diplomatic when it comes to conducting business."

"Yeah, we can trade stories about Nico all day, but the clock is ticking. So, do you know what room he's in?"

"It's the top floor, The Grand Suite. Let me write down the room number."

"Damn, he really is doing it big. Are you sure he's there?"

"I told my man to hit me if he bounced, and I haven't got a call, so yeah, he's there."

"Cool. So are you gonna wait down here for me?"

"How long do you think you'll be?"

"Maybe an hour or so."

"Take your time. Just hit me when you're done. I'll be in the neighborhood. But remember you have a flight to catch."

"No need to remind me. I can't miss that flight," I said, thinking about all the over-the-top lies I would have to come up with to appease Supreme.

When I entered the hotel, the soaring central atrium opened up to a fleet of luxurious guestrooms, a sexy lounge, and a polished cocktail bar with an adjoining restaurant. I was tempted to take a detour to the bar, but reminded myself that time wasn't on my side.

As I made my way closer to Nico's room, not knowing

what his reaction would be to seeing me again had me a little nervous. When I got to the door I put my ear against it to see if he had company. I heard what sounded like a television, but that was it. I knocked and waited for a few, but got nothing. I knocked again, this time harder, and heard movement. I could hear who I assumed was Nico at the door and I figured he was looking out the peephole to get a visual, but I was standing to the side so he couldn't see me.

"Who is it?"

I instantly recognized Nico's voice. "It's me, Precious." He opened the door, and just like that the nervousness vanished and a sense of comfort took its place.

"I can't believe you're here! How did you find me?"

"Do I have to explain in the hallway, or can I come inside?"

"My fault, please come in. But first, you have to show me some love." Nico held his arms open, and I welcomed the embrace. His hold had the same spellbinding effect it did the last time I felt him, as did his intoxicating scent.

After closing the door, he took my hand and led me to the spacious, slick, minimalist-inspired haven. The soothing natural colors and rich textures were showcased the moment you stepped on the soft wool carpeting. It was fitted to be chic, but with maximum comfort. The stunning panoramic views of New York and beyond were the icing on the already delectable cake.

After sizing up the ambiance of the room, I focused my attention on the scenery before me. Nico still captured the essence of a true G. His flawless mahogany skin was no longer highlighted by the cornrows he had grown last time I saw him. It was back to a low cut, full of jet-black curls. His six-two frame was solid, and his full lips were still decorated with a set of perfect white teeth. He was as fine as the day he swooped me up on 125th Street in Harlem years ago. "It's been too long, Nico."

"It sure has, baby girl. You're the last person I thought would be knocking at my door. You haven't yet told me how you found me."

"I hired someone to track you down."

"Interesting. What is so important for me to know that you felt the need to track me down? Before you answer that, how 'bout we go to the rooftop terrace and have a drink?"

"I would love that, I really would, but I have a flight to catch."

"Leaving so soon?"

"Yeah, I have to get back to LA."

"I can't lie. I was surprised when I heard you were living in Beverly Hills. Do you remember the first time I took you to Rodeo Drive? I'll never forget the smile on your face when you realized a street like that existed. I loved how everything was new to you back then. You were like a little girl discovering a whole other world."

"It's funny you mention that, because right before I came up here I reminisced about the very same thing."

"You're no longer that little girl, but then again, you never really were. I bet you don't remember what I said to you that night on our first date when we went to the park."

"Yes I do. I've never forgotten."

"I don't believe you. Tell me."

"You said I had the same darkness in my eyes as you,

and you never met a woman or a man besides your father that had that look."

"I was wrong, you do remember. But that was a lifetime ago. I know you have a flight to catch, so tell me what brings you back to NYC," he said, changing the subject.

Nico sat down on a chair and I took a seat on the couch across from him. I paused, trying to find the right words to use, but there was no easy way to say that someone wanted you dead. "There's no correct way to say this, but someone wants you dead and I came to warn you."

Nico sat quiet for a few minutes, and his demeanor remained intact. He was taking the news surprisingly well. "When you say someone wants me dead, do you mean there's a ransom on my head?"

"I wouldn't say a ransom. It's more like the person hired someone to take you out. It's was supposed to be done a few weeks ago, but some shit came up and it was postponed. I want you to be careful, watch your back because I don't know when they'll be given the green light to strike."

"Are you going to tell me who it is? 'Cause obviously you know."

"Honestly, I prefer not to. It's not like the person is going to do it themselves, so you need to watch out for anybody or anything that seems suspicious. I know it might seem like I'm not giving you enough but…"

"No, you're actually telling me a lot," he said, cutting me off. "You're telling me that you still care a great deal about me, because I know you're going through a very difficult time right now. Your daughter has been kidnapped, but you managed to squeeze in a flight to NYC to give me a heads up."

"I guess the whole world knows about Aaliyah."

"Yeah, your husband is extremely high profile. I know you must have had to go through a great deal of maneuvering to make this trip happen without him finding out. But you've always been good at maneuvering—make that scheming."

"I don't know if I should take that as a compliment or be offended."

"How about we call you resourceful, which is a good thing. I do appreciate the information and I'll do some asking around. I'm sure once that happens I'll find out who it is you're protecting."

"I'm not protecting anybody. I don't want you dead, that's all. Can't we leave it at that?"

"Out of respect for you, I'll leave it alone. I want to ask you about something much more important anyway."

"What?"

"I know you heard that Mike escaped from prison. Is he the one that kidnapped your daughter?"

"How did you know?"

"I didn't, but you have now confirmed it for me. I can't believe that nigga would do something that foul. That was never his style. Shit has really changed. But then again, I never thought it would be his style to rape you. When I read about that in the paper I wanted to show up at his trial and slice him open myself."

"I had a tough time dealing with that, but Supreme helped me through it. He was so good to me."

"I'm glad to hear that, although I wish I could've been there for you too, or better yet, been there to protect you from Mike. How did you find out it was him who kidnapped your daughter?"

"He called and bragged about it. He's a sick fuck. I guess he hasn't been in touch with you."

"Hell no! That nigga knows not to bring that bullshit my way. He would definitely be carried out in a body bag. I'd lullaby that nigga like he had snatched my own seed. The police don't have any leads?"

"Barely. You know how whack the cops can be. Supreme's working on a couple of leads, but the shit is moving so damn slow. I want my daughter home. It's killing me that she's with that fuckin' monster."

"If I find out anything that will help, you know I'll let you know."

"I know you will. We've been through some real live bullshit, but you've always been good people. That's why I'm happy to see you're still maintaining," I said, nodding my head in approval over the digs he was staying in.

"I'm making a few moves on the streets and business investments at the same time. I gotta try and hustle this game before it hustles me. I'm lucky to get a second chance, so I'm trying to make the most of it. I've learned a lot."

"What have you learned?" I was curious to know, since Nico always seemed on top of his game for the most part.

"How the drug game should be a Fortune 500 company. It's crazy how white men move way more drugs than us, but we're the ones that always get snatched up and locked down. It's set up that niggas on the bottom of the totem pole and the ones at the very top always get popped. The game is fixed so that you can only reach a certain level and your time is up. A big factor in that is the access white men have to money laundering. They have the type of relationships and connections to have their shit so clean it's damn near impossible to take them down. All a nigga can do is get a barber shop, beauty and nail salon, invest in some real estate properties, or try to open a car dealership. You can't legitimize hundreds of millions of dollars with that type of bullshit. We can't even buy paintings worth millions of dollars without every federal agency in the world knocking on our doors."

"I never thought about that before."

"You have no reason to. Supreme's making legitimate money and I commend him for that. A nigga like me wanna live the life of the rich and famous based off of street dreams. But if I want to have children and grow old watching my grandchildren come into this world, I have to minimize my street dreams. I can still be rich, just not filthy rich," he laughed.

"I feel you. I didn't put any value on preparing for a future until after having Aaliyah. That's when my priorities changed a lot. Before, I was quick to jump into some bullshit without giving a damn. Now I stop and think about the consequences. You know I'm still gonna jump in, but with more caution."

"Caution is good."

"Damn, I can't believe how much time has gone by," I said, looking down at my watch. "I hate to bring you bad news and run, but I have to go."

"Not a problem. But you know if you were able to find out I was in New York and where I was staying, then you could've easily gotten my number and called me with this information you have, instead of making a long trip."

"You're right. The truth is I wanted to see you again." Nico stood up and reached his hand out to me. I didn't hesitate to grab it. He lifted my chin and gazed into my eyes like he did so many times in the past. He used to call it his way of looking inside of my soul. Then his soft lips invaded mine, and I couldn't lie, the chemistry between us hadn't diminished and I wanted to give into the lust of the flesh.

"I'm glad you did because I've wanted to be with you again since the last time we were together," he said, breaking the momentum of our kiss for a moment before diving right back in with even more intensity.

"I can't," I said, pulling away. "This is an example of jumping in but thinking about the consequences. That kiss is the furthest this can go. You're my first love, Nico. I'll always have a soft spot for you, but I'm in love with my husband."

"Enough said. But here, take my number in case you ever need me—not for anything intimate, but as a friend."

"Thank you, and I want you to take my number too, you know, if you find out anything that can help bring Aaliyah home."

"I meant to tell you, I think it's a beautiful thing that you named your daughter after your mother. If she was alive she'd be so proud."

"Wow, I can't believe you remembered my mother's name. Most of the time I referred to her as the 'crack head' to you. I feel a great deal of shame in that now that I'm a mother. You know she had turned her life around before she got killed. I was so proud of her."

"Precious, it's okay. We've all said and done things to our parents we regret or wish we could take back. But trust me, before your mother left this earth she knew how much you loved her and only wanted the best for her. You've honored her name by passing it on to her grandchild. Let it go. It's all love."

The compassion Nico was showing for my mother made me for a brief second want to confide that Aaliyah could very well be his daughter just as easily as Supreme's, or unfortunately, Mike's. But what would be the point? Supreme was Aaliyah's father and it was best that it stayed that way. I gave Nico one last hug goodbye before leaving.

I called Ricky on my way downstairs, and thank goodness he was already waiting. "I thought you were going to miss your flight," he said when I got in the car.

"It could've easily happened, but I need to get home to my husband, speaking of him, I have to place a call. No disrespect but I need for you to be completely silent."

"I'm on your clock," Ricky responded, giving one of his player smiles.

I called Supreme and waited for him to pick up, hoping he hadn't got hip to my lie.

"Hey, baby, I was about to call you," Supreme answered,

sounding like he was still sweet on me, and I was relieved.

"Hi. Sorry, I'm just checking in but these seminars go on for hours and it's hard to get a moment from these people."

"Are you enjoying yourself?"

"I wouldn't say enjoy, but I'm learning a lot."

You'll have to school me in on it when I get home.

"When will that be?"

"Hopefully no later than early in the morning. When are you coming home?"

"Baby, we have to hear three more people speak, so not for a few hours."

"Okay, well call me when you get home to let me know you're safe."

"I will. Did you have a chance to speak to Maya when you stopped at home?"

"Nah, I didn't see her. I checked her room but she wasn't there. Maybe she and Clip made up."

"Maybe, but I hope not. We need to find out if he is on Team Mike or Team Supreme first. Has any suspicious moves been made at that apartment yet?"

"Not yet. So far ain't been a red flag, but my men are watching carefully. They on it."

"Do you think Maya hipped Clip that we thought he was suspect?"

"I hope not. But that's your girl. What do you think?"

I pondered briefly before answering. "Not Maya, she's a little street soldier. She understands the importance of keeping your lips locked when it comes to certain situations, even when your man or ex-man might be involved."

"Then it's all good, and hopefully Maya is right and

Clip is on the up and up."

"True, but I have to get back inside. Ms. Duncan is waiting."

"Cool. Make sure you call me when you get home."

"I will. Love you."

"Love you too, baby." I hung up ready to exhale.

"You handled that like a pro. I wonder how my sister would feel being used as your alibi?"

"Is that a question? Because I know Ms. Duncan would have my back. She understands the concept of doing whatever you have to do to survive."

"Indeed, but it makes me wonder if whether I should be pleased or disappointed that I never found a woman like you to marry."

"What you mean by that?"

"What I mean is, I admire how you're able to keep your cool under intense situations, but it's also scary that you're able to lie with such ease to the man you exchanged vows with. It's a double-edged sword, because you would be an excellent partner on the streets. I'm just not sure if the same can be said in the partnership of marriage."

"Interesting analysis, but, umm, luckily I'm not your problem so you don't have to worry. On to more important things. How are we looking on time?"

"Not to worry, you'll make the flight."

"Good. I spent much more time with Nico than I had anticipated."

"You all had a lot of catching up to do." Ricky's monotone voice made it hard for me to understand if what he said was a question or a general statement, so I ignored it. Catching the vibe, Ricky came at me again. "So how did it go with Nico? Were you able to resolve everything?"

"There are some people in life you'll never be able to resolve everything with. Nico is that person for me. But I was able to see him face to face and deliver the warning, so that was an accomplishment. And of course I owe that to you, Ricky. Thank you."

"That's what I do."

"Yes indeed, and you're very good at it. Before I forget, although I doubt you would let me, this is for you." I handed him an envelope full of Benjamin Franklin's. "That should be more than enough to cover all your expenses."

"Thank you, but I wasn't worried. If you didn't hit me off this time around, I knew you were good for it."

"'Preciate the confidence, but I don't like to owe people, especially the ones I'm doing business with."

"You a shrewd woman, Precious Cummings."

"Mills," I corrected him.

"My fault, how could I forget you're a married woman." It sounded as if Ricky was being sarcastic, but I had a flight to catch so I didn't have the time to give a fuck one way or the other.

"Ricky, you can drop me off right here," I directed as he pulled up beside a yellow cab that was blocking the curb.

"Are you sure?"

"Hell yeah, you see what time it is, or were you so caught up in trying to read my psyche that you stopped checking the clock? Don't answer, I have to go."

"Call me when you land!" I heard Ricky yell out the window as I entered the American Airlines terminal.

When I arrived home from the LAX airport and didn't see any cars parked along the circular driveway, the tight knot in my stomach loosened up. Supreme rarely kept his car in the garage, and if he was using a driver the Bentley would be resting out front.

I took my time going inside replaying the day's events. It was like damn! One minute I was sitting in front of Nico at a New York city hotel suite reminiscing about the past, and now I was back in Cali having to deal with my reality—my daughter was kidnapped and I didn't know when she would be back home.

It was so hush when I got in the house you would've thought the place had been abandoned. I immediately began flicking on all the lights so it would feel as if life was in the room. I walked toward the kitchen to get something to drink. My eyes instantaneously became fixated on a beautiful bouquet of flowers adorning the glazed lava stone countertop upon entering the kitchen. I was drawn to the array of Vandella roses, white hydrangeas, blue muscari and pink Peony's… it was as if they were calling my name. *Finally, something to put a smile on my face, after all the bullshit and heartache, a wonderful gesture from my husband to take away all the pain if only for one moment*, I thought as I smelled the breathtaking arrangement.

I noticed the small white envelope with "Precious" written across and I opened it to read the card inside. Before digesting the first word written, horror seized me. A jet-black curl began descending as it made its way out when I opened the card. I fell to the floor, banging my knees in an attempt to catch the locks. I preferred the hair to find a resting-place in the palm of my hand rather than on the cold marble beneath me.

"My baby! My poor baby!" was all I kept saying. I could distinguish Aaliyah's jet black curls from any head of hair. I ran my fingers through each strand on countless occasions. She was my baby, my pride and joy. To let it hit the ground was the same as me letting her die.

THE MESSAGE

"Supreme, come home right now!" I screamed in the phone. I could hear loud music in the background so I knew he was at the studio grinding, but fuck whatever he was working on. This was too much. I needed my husband home now.

"Baby, what's wrong?"

"That motherfucka's dead! He don't know it yet, but he's dead!"

"Precious, what the fuck is going on... talk to me?"

"When I got home there was a bouquet of flowers waiting for me. I thought they were from you."

"I ain't send you no flowers."

"I realized that once I opened the card."

"Who the fuck was they from...?" Supreme asked then immediately jumped to answer. "I know that nigga, Mike's punk ass didn't send you no fuckin' flowers and shit. Oh hell no, tell me I'm buggin'."

"It's worse than that."

"What, the nigga delivered that shit himself," he

countered, thinking that was as bad as it could get.

"I don't know who the fuck delivered them 'cause I wasn't here, but even if he had, it's still worse."

"Tell me what the fuck it is!" Supreme barked, ready for World War 3.

"Inside the envelope was a lock of Aaliyah's hair." On that note the line went dead. I kept trying to call Supreme back, but after the sixth time with no answer I knew this wasn't a dropped call situation. He hung the fuck up. I couldn't blame him. He was probably so pissed off that his only alternative was to shut the conversation down.

Still holding on to what represented to me a small piece of my daughter, I opened up the card again to read what the sick fuck had written, but it was blank. I guess Mike figured the message he wanted to send was made loud and clear, and he was right. It didn't matter that Vernika was dead or that Supreme had Donnell prisoner somewhere, Mike was very much in control. He was running the show, and we were just hapless ticket holders sitting front row waiting to see how the movie would end.

I heard the front door opening and I knew it was too soon for Supreme to get home, but before my mind started getting the best of me, I heard a familiar voice call out, "Is anyone home?" Maya echoed.

I rushed out the kitchen, needing to see a comforting face. "Maya, I'm so glad it's you. Where have you been?"

"Girl, tryna work it out with my sorry-ass boyfriend, but that's another Bronx Tale. What's going on with you? You look even more stressed than normal, is everything okay... oh shit! Mike calling harassing you again?"

I rolled my eyes up in the air, shaking my head before giving Maya the update. "This fool's reaching out through flower deliveries now."

"Excuse me?"

"Yeah, when I got home what I thought was a sweet gesture from my husband turned out to be poison from your brother."

"Mike sent you some flowers? How you know they were from him?"

"Because the card was blank except for a lock of Aaliyah's hair. Mike is the only loco nigga that would do some fucked up shit like that."

"Yo, that nigga had some flowers delivered with Aaliyah's hair in the card—he's lost his mind. I can't believe we share the same fuckin' DNA," Maya said, looking baffled.

"Have you been with Clip since you left here yesterday?"

"Yeah. What, you thinking he had a hand in this madness? Nah, he been on lock with me the whole time, and I swear I ain't see that nigga do nothing suspect—not no discreet phone conversations or nothing. I've been all up in his grill until I left his ass a minute ago."

"I need to find out who the fuck delivered this shit. The name of the florist is on the card, but of course they closed right now. They may have some valuable information."

"That's true. Did you call Supreme?"

"Yeah, I'm hoping he'll be home any minute."

Just then the front door opened. It was my husband and he had Detective Moore with him. This shit must have had Supreme real shaken if he let the police in on what happened.

"Where are the flowers and the hair?" Supreme asked, keeping it straight and to the point.

"In the kitchen…"

Before I could say another word, both Supreme and the detective breezed past me. I decided to stay on their trail, and Maya followed behind me. They were already dissecting the goods by the time we caught up.

"I already have officers getting in touch with the owner of the shop to see if we can get any leads. Because it's so late, they may not be able to find out anything until first thing in the morning, but they're on it," I heard Detective Moore explaining to Supreme.

"One of their delivery guys definitely dropped them off because he got clearance at the front gate and left them with one of my security guards. He had the proper identification, so the guard had no reason to be suspicious."

"Do you have any other hair samples of your daughter so we can compare it to what was sent in the envelope?"

"Detective, I know that's my daughter's hair. I don't need no comparisons," I spoke up, tired of listening from the sidelines.

Detective Moore turned his attention to me as if all of the sudden my presence was felt. He rubbed his stubby fingers through his own short, spiked, flaming red hair as if at a lost for words. "I'm sure you know your daughter's hair, but for legal reasons it's always better if we can prove it without leaving the slightest doubt. Mr. Owens will be brought to justice, and proving he sent your daughter's hair using a bouquet of flowers as a disguise will not sit well with jurors in any court of law."

Detective Moore's words were fine, and I even pretended to agree to what he was saying, but he was clueless. That so-called court of law he was preaching about was meaningless. Yeah, Mike would be brought to justice, but it wouldn't be by some pompous prosecutor and some drained ready-to-go-home jurors. Street justice, which equaled a torturous death was the only appropriate sentencing for Mike, and it would be carried out by me and me alone. "That's not a problem. I'm sure I have some hair strands in one of her baby brushes."

"I appreciate the cooperation, Mrs. Mills. I know this has to be extremely difficult for you. I'm happy that you and your husband are turning to me for help. I know you might feel we're not doing enough and you can handle it on your own, but when you're dealing with lowlifes like Mr. Owens, you need the law enforcement on your side. That's what we're here for, to help and bring your daughter home."

I knew the detective was sincere with his hero speech, but it sounded like recycled bullshit to me. I briefly thought about all the parents who heard this same dialogue when their child went missing and how they latched onto every word, praying their little one would be brought home to them alive. It wasn't until they got the knock on the front door from a couple of detectives like Moore, wearing cheap suits and smelling of stale cigarettes, that reality punched them in the face. Their child wouldn't be coming home. But instead of beating the detectives' asses for not delivering on the promises made for a safe return of their child, they had to stand and listen to the bullshit condolences.

I refused to let that be the fate of my family. I was born a fighter and would die one if it came to that. "Maya, will you go upstairs and get Aaliyah's brush from her bedroom? It should be on top of the dresser right next to her crib."

"No problem, I'll be right back."

"Are you Maya Owens, Mike's sister?" Detective Moore asked, bringing Maya to a halt.

"Yes, I am."

"I've needed to speak with you, but I had some difficulty tracking you down."

"Here I am. What did you need to speak to me about?"

"Your brother. Do you have any idea where he might be hiding out? Does he have any friends or family in the area he would turn to for help?"

"I haven't had any contact with Mike since he got locked up. To me, I no longer have a brother. The brother I knew is dead."

"I understand. Well, if you can think of anything, please give me a call," he said, handing Maya his business card. Maya put the card in the back pocket of her jeans and exited the kitchen.

My eyes then darted over to Supreme, who had been on mute for a while. He was standing over the flowers with his arms folded, and seemed to be in deep thought. As if he could sense me sizing him up, his eyes met up with mine. "Detective, I believe we've handled everything here. I'll be waiting for your call in the morning about what your officers were able to find out from the florist," he said to the detective, but somehow still able to keep his eyes on me. The shit was bizarre. I couldn't fathom what the fuck was going on his head.

"I will. I can show myself out. If it's not a problem, I'll wait in the foyer for Ms. Owens to bring down your daughter's hair sample."

"Please do so."

It wasn't until the detective extended his hand out to Supreme that he finally stopped eyeballing me like he was crazy. After shaking Supreme's hand, he picked up the vase of flowers after putting on a pair of surgical gloves, and was ready to break out.

"Umm, Detective Moore, where are you going with those flowers?" I stepped forward feeling territorial.

"Mrs. Mills, I have to take these flowers with me. This is evidence for our case."

"Oh, that's a shame. I was looking forward to shredding that poisonous greenery and tossing it out with the rest of the trash, but what you need it for is much more important, so please, take it."

Detective Moore gave me an awkward grin as if perturbed by what I said. He gave Supreme and I a half-hearted goodbye and finally got the fuck out of our faces.

Once the detective was ghost, I turned my attention to Supreme. "Why were you giving me the eye like I had caught the vapors or some shit?"

Supreme sucked his teeth and rested his elbows on the counter. "Something seems off to me."

"What you mean off? I told you how everything went

down with them damn flowers."

"It ain't the flowers, it's something else."

"Something else like what? You talking in riddles and shit."

"I can't put my finger on it, but shit is all off. Why did you get home so late?"

"I told you them church seminars be lasting damn near all night. Then I had to take Ms. Duncan back to her hotel, and she wanted me to stay and talk to her for a while. I mean, I didn't want to be rude, she did come here all the way from Brooklyn."

"What hotel is she staying at?" Supreme decided he wanted to get all Sherlock Holmes on me.

"Oh, mofo, I know you ain't tryna grill me like you po-po. I bring my ass home to some fucked up flowers with my daughter's hair lingering inside, and you want me to tell you where Ms. Duncan is laying her head at? If you really want to know, I stashed her in the Four Seasons in Beverly Hills. Here, since you obviously don't believe me, call the hotel," I said. grabbing the phone and shoving it in his face. praying that motherfucker didn't call my bluff. "What the fuck you waiting for? You want me to dial the number?"

Supreme put his hands up pushing the phone out his face. "I don't need to call and check your story."

"I think you do, because this trust shit is becoming more of an issue every fucking day, and I don't need the fucking stress. You tryna fault me for spending my day getting some spiritual guidance with Ms. Duncan, that's fucked up."

"Ain't nobody tryna fault you. I was picking up some vibes that was saying some shit wasn't adding up. I was wrong and I'm sorry."

I was about to keep the shit going to make him feel worse, but I knew better and backed off. I felt if I told him to call the Four Seasons one more time, he might just take me up on my offer and my lies would be exposed. "No need to be sorry, baby. We both going through heavy shit right now, and we don't need petty bullshit coming between us." I rubbed Supreme's shoulders, mitigating his hostility. He closed his eyes seeming to relax.

"Hey, is everything cool in here?" Maya asked, sneaking up on us.

"We're good. Did Detective Moore leave?" I wanted to know.

"Yeah, he bounced. I hope he finally gets a break in this case, 'cause Mike is wilding out. That nigga needs to be stopped… like yesterday."

"Who you telling? That nigga's like a bad venereal disease that keeps coming back. Can we please find a medication to zap this shit once and for all?"

"If it was only that simple," Supreme added. I could feel the tension creeping back in his shoulders.

"If only, is right. Well, I'm heading to bed. A bitch is tired."

"Did Clip wear that ass out?" I pried.

"No, I wouldn't let him stick his dick nowhere up in me—yet."

"I like how you added that yet at the end. That means he is this close" I raised up my thumb and index finger, putting a small space in between them, "To getting back inside the domain. I hope you know what you're doing."

"Honestly, Precious, I don't. What I do know is I don't want Destiny sniffing after my man, draped on his arm walking down the red carpet. If ain't gon' be me in that photo op posing with the designer getup and dripping with ice, it sho' ain't gon' be her trick ass. It won't be happening in this lifetime, and not the next if I have anything to do with it."

All I could do was shake my head at her. That was the immature young girl in her yapping. Hell, I had been there a few times in my life, and the only way you learn is going through the bullshit yourself. I mean, I didn't have no problem with Maya earning her battle scars going to war with Clip, as long as he didn't have nothing to do with helping Mike. More and more I was beginning to think that maybe I jumped the gun accusing him. He hadn't made any foul moves, and Supreme hadn't gathered any dirt on him. Maybe he was no more than a man-whore, getting his dick wet off of instant fame and nothing else. If that was the case, this was a problem Maya could handle on her own, because I had bigger issues that superseded pussy dilemmas.

"Well, handle your business, mama. But you know if you need me, I got your back."

"Thanks, Precious. I can always count on you. Good-night you guys."

"Goodnight," Supreme and I said in unison.

"I'm tired myself. I had a long day. I'ma head to bed. Are you coming?" I asked Supreme.

"I'll be up shortly. I have to go to my office and make some phone calls. But I'm coming."

"Okay, baby." I gave him a kiss on the lips and went upstairs. I was exhausted, physically and mentally. There seemed to be no end insight to this madness. When I got to the bedroom, I fell on the bed needing to rest my drained body before taking a shower. I wanted to turn on the television and see if Aaliyah's kidnapping was still headlining news, or if was she fading into the background, being overshadowed by more current events.

I scanned the room for the remote control, but it wasn't on the dresser or the nightstand, so I got down on my hands and knees in search of the gadget. Oh shit! I forgot all about slimy-ass Vernika's purse. Last night I was so busy trying to hide shit from Supreme that it slipped my mind that I stashed the shit under the bed. I never did have a chance to finish going through her mess, although I doubt anything of importance is in there.

I tossed Vernika's purse down and noticed the remote at the foot of the bed. I clicked on the television and turned to Nancy Grace while rummaging through the purse once again. The second time around proved fruitless. I then noticed a small black wallet in what appeared to be an almost secret compartment on the side of the bag. I opened the wallet up and there was a few hundred dollars inside, a tiny bag of what looked to be cocaine, and a folded up piece of paper that had been ripped off a notepad. I opened up the paper and it had an address scribbled down. It didn't have the city or state, just the zip code, which was all the navigation system needed. I had a feeling it was located right here in the LA area. A smile crept across my face, because I believed I might've gotten a tad bit closer to discovering the vaccine to that hard to get rid of venereal disease.

ONCE AGAIN IT'S ON

I woke up ready for war. Besides the heat I would be packing, my most powerful ammunition was the address I found in Vernika's purse. How the piece of paper was all neatly tucked away in Vernika's purse, I knew it meant that shit was important. And besides doing Mike's dirty work, what else could've been that significant in her life? With the address now in my pocket for safe keeping, I laced up my Timberland boots, anxious to hit the streets.

"Baby, where you off to dressed in gear more suitable for the hoods in New York?" Supreme asked, standing in the entrance of our bedroom door.

"I have a few things to take care of, that's all." I kept it real nonchalant so he wouldn't start with the interrogation.

"This early in the morning, what you gotta do?"

I guess I wasn't nonchalant enough, because here he was with the next question.

"Ms. Duncan's leaving today so I wanted to tell her bye before she left. I need to pick up some clothes from the cleaners that's way overdue... you know, take care of shit like that. I mean is that a problem?"

"No, I was just hoping maybe I could go out and have a nice breakfast with my wife. With all the bullshit going on, we haven't had much alone time. I think we need to reconnect."

"I feel you on that, Supreme, but until we bring Aaliyah home I think we got bigger problems than reconnecting."

"That's not what I'm saying. I know having breakfast in a restaurant ain't gon' change our circumstances, but at least it will make me feel as if we still united. I've lost my daughter, but I don't want to lose my wife too."

"Supreme, don't say no shit like that. We ain't lost Aaliyah," I said, rising up from the chaise. "You talking as if all hope is lost in bringing our daughter home, and that's some bullshit." I was now within spitting range of Supreme, ready to stick my Timberland boot up his ass for even insinuating that my baby was gone forever.

"Precious, I give you my word I didn't mean it like that." Supreme held on to my hands with a firm grip as he continued. "What I said came out wrong. On everything I love, I know we bringing our baby home but I'm talking right now in the present tense and what the situation is at this moment. At this very second we have lost our daughter, and I'm only trying to hold on to you as tightly as possible, because until we bring her home, you're all I have. Believe it or not, your presence is giving me the strength to get up every morning and fight this shit without losing my mind."

Ring...ring...ring...

Supreme's cell phone went off before I had a chance to respond to what he said, but that was a good thing because I really didn't know what my comeback would be.

"Hello… What…? How the fuck that happen…? Stay right there, I'm on my way," Supreme said, and flipped his cell shut.

"Who was that? What happened?" I questioned, perplexed by Supreme's agitation after his phone call.

He ignored me and damn near sprinted to his walk-in closet to a safe that used a fingerprint scan for access. He pulled out two weapons from his arsenal of guns, and had "I'm on a mission, so move the fuck outta the way" etched on his face.

"Supreme, where are you going? And don't ignore me."

"Some shit went down at the spot where Donnell is holed up and I have to go handle it."

"Fuck that, I'm coming with you," I said, grabbing my belongings, ready to be all up in the mix.

"Let me handle this. You go do whatever you had planned this morning and I'll hit you later on."

"You can either let me come with you or I'ma find my own way. But regardless, I will be knee-deep in this shit."

From the keen expression on my face, Supreme knew I was not budging and he wouldn't win this argument. "I don't have time to debate this shit with you, so come on."

When Supreme pulled up to the small one-story brick house nestled in the cut, I wondered how he ever found this spot. During the drive, he took so many crazy-ass turns that I couldn't remember how the fuck we got here, or even what part of LA we were in. Not once during the ride did Supreme tell me what had gone down at this hideout, but from how quickly he put the Range in park and jumped out the driver's side, I knew it was some heavy shit.

"Damn, can I at least get out the passenger side before you jet off?"

"You the one who was dying to be shotgun, so keep up," Supreme cracked, not breaking his stride.

I stepped up my pace, sizing up my surroundings at the same time. Nothing in the desolate area stood out. There weren't even any houses nearby. The only neighbors on either side were dirt and grass.

"I see why you got Donnell stored in here. I mean can't nobody see or hear shit in this fucking area," I said as I finally caught up to Supreme. As we walked up the long dirt walkway, two of his watchdogs were standing outside the front door, waiting.

"Now what the fuck happened?" Supreme said, brushing past the two armed guards dressed in the prerequisite all black uniform.

"We don't know how this shit happened. We pulled up about an hour ago to relieve Chris from the night shift, and this what we found."

When we walked into the open space, my eyes immediately darted to the blood splatter that greeted us on the far wall directly in our line of vision. A man was tied up in a chair with his arms cuffed behind his back and ankles chained. His one-time white wife beater was now crimson red from the bullet that penetrated his chest. But wanting to guarantee that all life was ceased, the shooter put one shot through the head, spraying brain tissue on the walls.

"Let me guess. The dead man is Donnell Graham."

Three pairs of eyes leered at me with disdain, as if I had been the one who had infiltrated their secret operation.

"Where's Chris?" Supreme asked, waiting for the two men to lead the way. They guided us to a bathroom in the hallway. When one of them pushed opened the door, Chris was sitting on the toilet holding a trashy magazine with big booty chicks spreading they're shit in all sorts of creative positions. I hoped he was able to get his shit off and bust a nut before the shooter put that ass to sleep with the clear shot through the mouth.

"Fuck!" Supreme belted, damn near leaving a hole in the bathroom wall from a potent punch. "I can't believe this shit. How the fuck did someone get up in here and take out Chris and that piece of shit?"

"We trying to figure that shit out too. We talked to Chris about one in the morning and everything was cool."

"Why was he here by himself with no backup?"

"The last few nights Devon was sharing the nightshift with Chris after you took him off of driving duty. Then a couple of days ago, Chris started letting Devon leave a little after midnight, saying there was no sense in both of them staying all night."

"What?" Supreme stormed out of the bathroom agitated. The watchdogs were a step behind, trying to explain how the shit got all fucked up, leaving his top man and his potential informant deceased.

"Chris felt he could hold down the late night shift on his own. He said they didn't need two bodies to watch a chained man sleep all night. I guess he was wrong."

"Yeah, Einstein, I guess so. Has either of you spoken to Devon?" Supreme questioned, shaking his head in frustration.

"No. We've been calling him since we got here, but his phone keeps going straight to voicemail. I even called his crib, but no answer."

"That shit don't make no sense. Everybody knows they supposed to be available at all times. Send one of the men to his crib and find out what the fuck is going on. I hope whoever did this ain't got Devon tied up some fuckin' where. A crew of niggas coulda ran up in here for all we know. But how in the hell did they find this spot?"

"Yeah, that's what I want to know, 'cause ain't nobody accidentally running up on this joint. You need some serious assistance finding it. My brain damn near turned to mush trying to remember all the twists and turns you took getting here. The shooter had some help... an inside job kind," I added.

The hired goons instantly went on the defense. "Supreme, we ain't have nothing to do with this. Chris was our boss and we followed his orders."

"No, motherfuckers, *I'm* your boss. Nobody should've been working this shift alone without clearing it with me first. I don't give a fuck what Chris told you. Now look, that nigga's dead, Devon's MIA, and we lost our only link to finding Mike. I pay ya niggas top dollar to fuckin' babysit and you can't even do that shit properly. What the fuck is this world coming to when grown-ass men with guns can't even keep a chained down nigga in a chair alive? Fuck!"

There was nothing more pathetic then watching two big-ass burly niggas sulking in the corner like scorned bitches. I wanted to tell them clowns to man-up, but it wouldn't have changed the grim circumstances.

"Listen, get this shit wrapped. Call in the cleaning crew and have these bodies disposed of. You know what else to do," Supreme stated, shooing his measly workers along with repulsion. "Then get everybody together, because we having a meeting tonight at the other spot to discuss the ramifications from this bullshit operation you niggas fucked up."

I stood in the back listening as Supreme gave his orders. For the first time I saw him in a completely different light. It was a bombshell to come to grips with the fact that Supreme was a killer just like Nico, Mike and me. He ordered his men to call in a cleaning crew with such ease that this clearly wasn't the first or even the second time he'd done so. His request was as second nature to them as pulling out their dick and taking a piss. How did I miss this about my husband? I always saw him as some dude from the hood that made good by breaking into the music industry. Never a cold-blooded killer who could dispose of bodies the way the average person tosses out trash. In my mind, Supreme was different from me. He didn't share the darkness that loomed over me. When he turned to kill-or-be-killed tactics, I assumed his survival instincts had kicked in and he was trying to save and protect his family. I didn't doubt that was the driving force behind this particular situation, but what about the ones I knew nothing about? And something told me there were many.

My mind then jumped to Nico and the hit Supreme had put out on him. Even with that, I felt there was some sort of reasonable explanation. Maybe Supreme never forgave Nico for shooting me and killing the child I was carrying, and he wanted retribution. I had to give my husband the benefit of the doubt. Although I wanted Nico alive, Supreme had to feel justified in wanting him dead.

"Let's go," I heard Supreme say, snapping me out of the distant places my mind had gone. It was then I noticed the watchdogs conducting business on their BlackBerry's, no doubt executing the orders from their boss.

When we got outside, I reached my hand out to Supreme. I wanted to feel if there was any warmth left in him. It was strange because I felt as if I no longer knew the man I was married to, but at the same time he was still my husband and I yearned to connect with him. That's why what flowed from my lips next seemed necessary.

"Baby, I think we might have one more lead that can put us back on Mike's trail," I said, sliding my fingers in the grasp of his hands. Originally, I was going to follow this probable come-up on my own, but this was the way to reconnect with Supreme. I did, however, need to pretend that I wasn't confident with the lead so he wouldn't catch on that only in the last thirty seconds I decided to bring him in on my undertaking. "I could be wrong and it might lead to nothing, but of course I wanted to share it with you."

"What lead? The two leads we had are dead and ain't no bringing them back."

"But sometimes even the dead find ways of speaking to you." I reached in my pocket and took out the piece of paper and handed it to Supreme.

"What are you giving me this for?"

"Open it."

Supreme stopped a few feet away from his Range Rover and unfolded the yellow paper. He stared down for a second and looked back up at me. "Okay, this is the address to…"

"This morning I was going through Vernika's purse and I found that paper tucked away real discreet. At first I didn't think anything of it, but maybe it's a secret location that Mike gave her." I had to switch up the time that I found the paper, because Supreme would be ready to get up in my ass for the delay in bringing it to his attention.

"This morning? But that shit went down with Vernika a few days ago. Why are you just now giving me this?"

"With Ms. Duncan and the church conference and all the other bullshit, I didn't have time to go through her purse until this morning."

"Oh, now I get it. So when you were lacing up those Timbs," he said, pointing down to my boots, "Like you was going to rumble through the jungle, tracking down this address was the real errand you were running."

"No. I was already planning on hitting the street to run some errands. While I was getting dressed I remembered that I had Vernika's purse and I searched through it. I came across the piece of paper, glanced at it for a minute and put it in my pocket. Honestly, I didn't think anything of it. I was gonna tell you about it, but at that moment it wasn't that deep to me."

"So at what point did it become deep enough that you opted to let me know about it?"

"When we were in the house and you were chewing out them silly niggas in there, I put my hands in my pockets, felt this piece of paper and remembered this fucking address. With the dude, Donnell dead and all our leads dried up, although a crap-shoot, I figured it might lead to something." I paused for a second before continuing, trying to determine if Supreme believed my half-ass story. He was biting down on his lip, which wasn't an encouraging sign, but I thought, *Fuck it,* and kept it going.

"Listen, don't be mad. I've had so much shit on my mind that I got caught slipping. I shoulda been more focused and got on top of this a few days ago. But, baby, you know how stressed I been and I'm doing the best I can." I put my head down and let out a tender sigh, hoping to soften Supreme up.

"All I'm saying is with all this shit going on you can't let shit slip like this. Time is of the essence right now. From now on, if you come across any information, I don't care how bogus you think it might be, you bring that shit to me, understand?"

"I got you."

"Cool. Now let's go check this shit out. I'ma have a couple of my men meet us over there just in case we might need backup. I got a nine millimeter in the center console. You know how to work that?" Supreme lifted his chin up in my direction in anticipation of my response.

"Don't play, you already know I get down for mines." I slammed the passenger door, feeling like Bonnie to my nigga's Clyde.

"Precious, that ain't for you to play with," Supreme said, pressing down on the gas and driving off. "I don't know what we about to walk up in, so I want you to have some protection since we both know you ain't gon' sit yo' ass still."

"I'm not gonna fuck this up. I'll follow your lead." I sat back in the seat and closed my eyes. I couldn't shake the feeling that I was missing something. It was as if all the answers to my questions were neatly compiled in a sealed envelope waiting for me to open. But I kept losing track of the envelope's location. I wasn't focusing my attention on the right person who had all the answers to my questions. Different faces kept flashing in my head: Supreme, Maya, Clip, Nico, Devon, Ms. Duncan, Ricky, Anna, Detective Moore, even the dead, Vernika and Donnell. With everything inside of me, I believed one or more of these people knew all the moves Mike was making. I couldn't believe I threw my husband in the batch, but this was my daughter, and at this point I was looking at everybody cross-eyed.

In my mind I revisited past conversations with

each of them and tried to determine if there were any underlying messages that I was missing. The more I thought about it, the more it seemed that kidnapping Aaliyah wasn't Mike's ultimate goal. He had a much more sinister objective in mind, but what? Mike was a crazy motherfucka and there was no telling what lengths he would go to for revenge.

"Precious... Precious... Precious," I heard my name being called and then a forceful arm shaking me. I shook my head, opening my eyes. "What the fuck, did you fall asleep?" Supreme asked, turning off the ignition.

"I must've dozed off." I looked around and saw we were in an upscale apartment complex. "Where are we?"

"In Sherman Oaks, California."

"Could this be where Aaliyah has been all this time?" I wondered, sharing my thoughts out loud.

"Anything's possible, but that shit would be crazy, because she would've been right under our noses. But then again, how would we know that? I guess it's pretty easy to have a baby under wraps if you keep them indoors. But we might be getting way ahead of ourselves. This could be someplace a nigga that chick Vernika was creeping with stay at."

"True, but only one way to find out. Do you know the building number?"

"The apartment number is 6248, so I'm assuming it is building number six. Hold on a minute, let me call and see where the two men I told to meet us here are at."

While Supreme made his phone call, I scanned the place seeing if anything struck me as odd—a vehicle, person—anything. Nothing popped out, but I definitely didn't think this was a meeting spot for Vernika and some jumpoff.

"Let's go. They're going to meet us in front of the apartment building," Supreme said, getting out of the Range.

I opened the center console and grabbed the nine, making sure I was strapped for the unexpected. When we got to the lower level of building six, Supreme saw the apartment wasn't on that floor, so our legs swiftly made there way up their stairs. It wasn't until we'd gone through the entire flight of stairs and reached the very top that we found the apartment number, and standing against the wall waiting for us were Supreme's two men.

"It's about fucking time," I said, gasping for air. I knew I needed to hit the gym and start doing some cardio if I was tired from running up some damn stairs.

"Did you guys hear any activity going on in there?" Supreme asked the men leaning up against the door.

"No," one of the men answered.

I was noticing a pattern with Supreme's hired help. They all looked the fucking same: tall, black and muscular. I didn't understand how he could tell them apart, especially since their entire outfits were identical.

"Precious, you stand off to the side. I'ma knock on the door and wait a few to see if anyone answers. If don't nobody speak up or show their face, we busting the door down," Supreme directed.

I stood off to the side, hoping that no one would come out their apartment or pop up on the scene, interrupting us. It was a weekday in the middle of the afternoon, so most people were probably at work, but I didn't want any surprises. More importantly, I didn't want the police being called before we got the first crack at inspecting the apartment for clues.

Supreme knocked at the door and paused for a few seconds, then knocked again. "I don't hear shit in there." He turned to one of his men. "Yo, bust this shit open."

The man pulled out his gun with the silencer already attached and busted off two shots at the door lock, so he basically had to tap it for the shit to open.

When we stepped inside the place, it smelled of Linen & Sky Febreeze Air. The entrance opened into a living room with a butter-cream leather sofa set adorning the hardwood floor. An oval-shaped glass coffee table mounted on ivory stone rocks sat in the center, with magazines and books neatly stacked on top. Then, there it was, nestled in the far left-hand corner. A playpen. The first sign that a baby had been here—possibly mine.

Supreme's men made there way down the hallway to check the bedrooms, and I went over to the playpen, touching, looking and even trying to smell the scent of my Aaliyah.

"Supreme, I think you should come take a look at this," one of his men called out from the back.

While Supreme went to the back, I searched the kitchen and opened the cabinets to cans of Similac and baby bottles. The refrigerator had jars of baby food. "Supreme, a baby is definitely residing here," I said, walking down the hall to the bedroom Supreme was in. My mouth dropped at the pink paradise. The crib, dresser, changing table, rocking chair were all white with cotton candy colored walls and accessories. I went to the crib and rubbed my hands on the fitted sheets and picked up a cotton stuffed toy rabbit lying flat on the firm mattress. I then opened up the dresser drawers and found pull-on pants, coverall sets and socks. I held on to a floral print onesie and brushed it against my nose. It smelled of fresh baby detergent.

"Precious, no doubt a baby lives here, but we don't know if it's Aaliyah," Supreme reminded me, noticing that I was becoming lost in a world that might have not been that of my daughter.

"I know, but this can't be a coincidence. The sizes of these clothes would fit Aaliyah perfectly."

"That's not enough to convince me. We need more."

"I think we just found it," I said, staring at the rocking chair. I swallowed hard not wanting to get too excited.

"What...what did you find?" Supreme came closer to me, wanting to know what had me so transfixed.

I took a few steps closer to the rocking chair and gently grabbed the light-pink crochet trimmed cashmere blanket draped over the armrest. I turned over to the inside, and there lay the proof. Aaliyah's name was embroidered in the corner.

"This is the blanket Anna got. She always kept it with Aaliyah even when it was fucking hot outside."

Supreme grabbed the blanket from me, scrutinizing the validity of what I was saying. "I remember this blanket," he said, covering his face with it. For a moment I thought he was about to break down and cry. He stood there silent; the only thing I could hear was his heavy breathing. "Were you all able to find anything else?" he asked the men, finally coming up for air.

"There were a few clothes hanging in the closet and in the drawers… and this," the man said, handing Supreme a picture. "Maybe that's who the clothes belong to."

I instantly recognized the woman in the picture. "That's Destiny!" I squealed with repulsion.

"She do look mad familiar. Who the fuck is she and how you know her?" Supreme was dumbfounded.

"That's Destiny, the video chick that me and Maya caught Clip fucking around with."

"This is Clip's ho right here?" Supreme threw down the picture and balled up his fist. "Let me find out this nigga really got something to do with this bullshit!"

I picked the picture off the floor and stared at it again. Destiny was cheesed up, sitting on what appeared to be the same couch in the living room.

Supreme pulled out his cell.

"Who you calling?"

"That nigga, Clip. Fuck! He ain't picking up. Don't nobody want to answer they fuckin' phones today."

"Do you really think it's a good idea to confront Clip over the phone? Wouldn't it be better to see him face to face so he can't get slick and escape from us? More importantly, get ghost and not tell us where Aaliyah is? We don't need to fuck up anymore links to Mike," I contended. This was the first time since the nightmare begun that I truly felt we were close to bringing Aaliyah home, and I didn't want a hot tempered Supreme messing it up by alerting Clip over the phone that we were on to him.

"Let me put in a call to Maya just so we can see where Clip's at. Then we'll go to him. From there, I don't care if you hang that nigga upside down by his dick as long as he gets to telling us what we need to know. Clip's a soft nigga. He ain't gonna try to be no soldier like that cat, Donnell."

"You call Maya, and I want both of you to keep post right outside this apartment," Supreme said, pointing to his men in black. I have a feeling ain't nobody coming back to this crib, but it's best to be careful."

"Do you believe we should get Detective Moore involved? I mean he could get access from the leasing office that could be extremely helpful. Like who's name the apartment's in, who's paying the rent, bank information... just shit that they not gonna voluntarily tell us."

"You might be right, Precious. I'll give Detective Moore a call after we've gone over every nook and cranny and I feel satisfied we've obtained all the pertinent information we can get."

While Supreme and his men began rummaging through every inch of the apartment, I placed my call to Maya. She wasn't answering her phone either, and after the tenth try I decided to leave a message. "Hey Maya, this is Precious. Listen, umm, I need for you to hit me back as soon as you get this message. An emergency came up and I need your assistance, so get back to me ASAP."

After leaving the message on her cell, I called the crib and got nothing but the answering machine. I opted not to leave a message there not wanting to take any chances of raising suspicion with Clip.

"Were you able to get in touch with Maya?" Supreme asked, taking a break from his search.

"No, she's not answering her phone. It's like everybody's ghost today. This shit is crazy."

"Crazy don't begin to describe it."

"Did you find anything else?"

"Not really. Besides the clothes, there was a couple pair of shoes, toothpaste and bullshit like that."

"Where did homeboy find that picture of Destiny?"

"Inside one of the books that was in the drawer next to the bed. The broad was probably rushing so fast to break the fuck out and forgot she even left her picture there"

"Her forgetfulness is our gain. Shit, because without that picture of Destiny, there wouldn't have been anything to connect Clip. I want to get my hands on that trick so bad. I wish I had her fucking number. Besides Clip, do you know anybody else who might have an address or contact information on Destiny?"

"I'm already on it. I put in a call to my secretary to get in touch with the agent who cast the video to see if they had her shit on file. I'm waiting for her to get back to me now."

"Yeah, but we need Clip. That nigga is the one who got the answers. I doubt that simple-ass chick, Destiny knows a damn thing of real importance, like where the hell Aaliyah is at right now. Honestly, I just want an opportunity to beat her ass for being in the same crib my daughter was held captive at."

"Hold up, this my secretary now," he informed me before answering the call. "Hey Stacy, what did you find out for me?"

While Supreme was digging for feedback, I sat down on the loveseat, thinking back to that day Maya and I caught Destiny's trifling ass in bed with Clip. Damn, I wish I would've let Maya beat that ho down. Shit, I should've put my foot up her ass too. I'm trying to play nice with the trick and she was probably sitting up in this very spot sharing space with my child. Did Clip clue the silly trick in on the fact that the baby was that of Supreme's, or was she so stupid that she ran with whatever half-ass story he gave her? I guess we won't find that out until we found the tramp. "What did she say?" I asked when I saw Supreme hang up his phone.

"Not shit worthwhile. The address the casting agent has is a P.O. Box, and the number is one of those voicemail phone services."

"Fuck! It's like we keep hitting one brick wall after another."

"Who you telling? Shit, we don't even know how long ago whoever was staying here bounced."

"Yeah, but it couldn't have been that long ago, because besides the baby food jars, there was some leftover meatloaf in there, and a carton of milk that hasn't even been opened yet."

"Shit, we're just one step behind them then."

"I bet they bounced when they got word that Donnell had been jacked and Vernika was dead. Mike probably wasn't a hundred percent positive whether Donnell would roll over and start snitching or what else we would find out, so to be on the safe side he probably cleared house."

Supreme sat down next to me nodding his head. "That's logical. Not knowing exactly how much time he had on his hands, he probably decided not to fuck with the rest of the shit in the crib and just clear out where he was laying his head, not wanting to leave any direct evidence to him."

"So you think Mike was living here too? That nigga got balls."

"It would make sense. But he definitely had someone else with him, because he couldn't go outside or show his face and take a chance someone would recognize him."

"That someone else had to be Destiny. I mean, why else would there be women's clothes, shoes and shit, and that picture of her?" I reasoned.

"Destiny fucking Mike and Clip, it's plausible. They got their shared whore maintaining shit for them and carrying out baby duty."

"If she was fucking Mike in this crib, then she had to know he kidnapped Aaliyah. Damn, I wish I would've let Maya beat her ass and put in a couple of licks of my own. So what's next?"

"Besides the few items we found, the search of this place has come up empty so I think I'ma go ahead and place that call to Detective Moore. If I do it now while it's still business hours, he should be able to find out some viable information."

"Cool. While you stay here and wait for the detective, I want to take your car and drive by a couple of spots and see if I can locate Maya."

"I don't know about that. I think maybe we need to stick together."

"Supreme, there is no sense in both of us sitting here waiting for Detective Moore. We need to make the most out of all the time we have. While you're here, I might be able to find Maya and she could tell me where Clip is, but we know that's not going to happen with both of us sitting here. She's not answering her phone, and Maya is good for leaving that shit someplace, so she might not even have it with her."

Supreme kept shaking his head, not convinced that us going our separate ways was the answer.

"Listen, if I get in touch with Maya and she tells me where Clip is, I promise I'll call you before making a move."

"Precious, I don't want you to even tell Maya what we've found out until we get our hands on Clip. I know that's your girl, but she's still in love with that nigga. When I left a message for Clip, I told him it was important for him to get in touch with me over some music shit. That's the same line I want you to run on Maya."

"I can do that."

"But don't confront that nigga without me. He evidently ain't the loyal cat I pegged him to be, so ain't no telling what he's capable of."

"If I'm able to get in touch with Maya and I find out

anything, you're the first call I'll make. But make sure you hit me too if you come across any new leads."

"No doubt. But Precious, please be careful and don't try to be no hero. Our main objective is to bring our daughter home. One wrong move can fuck all that up."

I digested what Supreme said as I took the car keys from him. The comment he made about the one wrong move kept ringing in my ear. We were so close to putting the pieces to this puzzle together that making the wrong move was what I wanted to avoid at all costs.

WHO SHOT YA

Keyshia Cole's new single blasted from the speakers as I headed towards Maya's apartment. I put in a call to make sure she wasn't at my crib, but security informed me he hadn't seen her since leaving early that morning. As Keyshia poured her heart out about love and pain, my heart ached about the same. But it wasn't over a man, it was about my daughter.

I didn't share it with Supreme, but I thought about how if I had searched through Vernika's purse more thoroughly the very night she was killed, I might have found the address sooner and maybe got Aaliyah back then. But instead, I rushed off to New York to see Nico and forgot about the purse until a couple of days later. Those two days might have been crucial.

What if Mike didn't find out about Vernika's death immediately and lingered at the apartment for another day or so with Aaliyah? I knew I was doing a lot of speculating, but the guilt was weighing heavy on my mind. Was it necessary for me to see Nico in person, Couldn't I have just put in a phone call? It was too late to countdown the what if's. I did make the decision to get on a plane and warn Nico, and somehow I would have to make peace with that. And the only way that would happen was to bring my baby home.

"What the fuck!" I said, feeling a vibration on top of my thigh. I looked down and realized a call was coming from my cell. I had forgotten that I put my phone on vibrate, because I knew I wouldn't be able to hear it with my loud-ass music blasting. I turned down Keyshia and took the call. "Hello?"

"Precious, it's me, Maya."

"Girl, I've been trying to get in touch with you." I glanced at the number on the phone. "Where you calling me from?"

"It's a pay phone."

"A pay phone? Did you get the messages I left you on your cell?"

"No. I forgot my cell at your house. I haven't had that shit all day. But listen, I need you to meet me somewhere."

"Okay, I need to speak with you anyway. Supreme is looking for Clip. He has some important music shit to discuss with him. It's kinda urgent. Do you know where he is?"

"Precious, I need for you to come meet me now. We can talk about Clip when you get here… just come, please."

"Okay, give me the address," I said, typing it in the navigation system.

"How long is it going to take you to get here?"

"The navi' say about twenty minutes, but you know how I drive, so maybe ten, fifteen minutes."

"Okay, I'll be waiting out front in my car."

"Cool. I'll see you in a few."

Maya's voice sounded mad shaky and it had me concerned. She seemed stressed, and I figured it had to do with Clip. She had probably caught him fucking around again and was losing her mind. But that shit was nothing compared to the bullshit the nigga had really been up to. Although Maya had caught Clip red-handed with Destiny, she still remained his biggest supporter when it came to his loyalty for Supreme. She refused to believe my suspicions that Clip was a snake who would cross Supreme at the drop of a dime. You would think after being deceived by her own brother, who turned out to be the biggest loser of all, her judgment wouldn't be so blinded by Clip. I had to remind myself that even though she played the tough girl role, she was still young and impressionable. Nobody would want to believe the man they loved was capable of playing a role in the kidnapping of an innocent child. I hated to be the one to break the news to Maya that her man had done just that.

When I exited the highway, I made a left at the first light. I drove for a couple of minutes and the further I drove, the nonresidential street appeared more and more deserted. I eyed my navigation system to make sure I hadn't made a wrong turn, but I was following the directions correctly. I then took another left turn and continued to drive for a few more minutes until I heard the computer generated voice tell me I had reached my destination.

I turned into the isolated parking lot and saw what looked to be an abandoned warehouse. I didn't see Maya's car in the front, so I drove around the back. That's when I saw Maya's candy-apple red Jaguar, Clip's baby blue Benz with the vanity plates, and a black Navigator with pitch-black tint, but I didn't know who it belonged to. I pulled the Range next to Maya's car, but I guess she was inside the warehouse.

"What the fuck is Maya doing at a warehouse? Could she have found out that Clip is involved in Aaliyah's kidnapping and confronted him, and now the nigga is in there holding her hostage? But why wouldn't she have said something to me while she had me on the phone? Maybe she wanted to sit down and tell me to my face. Then Supreme's words started ringing in my ears again; *One wrong move can fuck that all up.*" "Let me call him right now so he can know what's going down," I said to myself.

"You find Maya?" Supreme asked, answering the phone and making it clear what was on his mind.

"As a matter of fact, I did."

"Jackpot! So where is Clip at?"

"They're at a warehouse."

"A warehouse, right now?"

"Yeah, and I'm worried about Maya. She called me from a pay phone and gave me this address to meet her at. She said she would be waiting in her ride, but she's not. Clip's car is here and somebody else's car, but I don't know who it belongs to. What if he's flipped out and is holding her hostage up in there?"

"Precious, you stay in the car and wait for me to get there. Don't go inside the warehouse. Wait in your car until I get there, do you hear me?"

"Yes. But what if Maya needs my help?"

"You ain't no good to Maya if you walk in there and get yourself killed. Stay fuckin' put. Now give me that address."

After I gave Supreme my location, he hung up the phone so quickly I didn't' even have a chance to say bye. I tapped my fingers on the steering wheel, wanting him to hurry up and get here. I mean, it was killing me to keep my ass in the car instead of going inside to see what was going down. If possible, it's always my preference to dig my hands deep in the mud and get dirty. Playing the waiting game wasn't one of my strong points. I kept looking down at my watch, and what seemed like an hour would only be one minute. I ruffled my fingers through my hair, with feelings of anxiousness and fear intertwining. I then took a few deep breaths so I could relax, and when it started working, that's when it turned bad.

The explosive sounds of gun shots were echoing from inside the warehouse. Without second-guessing myself, I grabbed my heat and jumped out the car. All I could think about was saving Maya. I wouldn't be able to live with myself if I let my girl die while I was playing it safe in my ride.

I ran up on the side door, but it was locked. I took off around the front and pushed open the door. It was eerily quiet when I got inside. I aimed my gun up ready to blast any motherfucka I even thought was wishing me harm. The dark walls and empty space gave it a dreadful appearance. It reminded me of a spot that would be perfect for torturing. The soles of my shoes lightly tapped the concrete flooring. I pivoted around a corner where a flickering light was coming from a room in the back. I paused, assessing the different prospects that lay behind the closed door. I continued to proceed towards my destination, saying to myself, *Shoot first ask questions later.* There was complete silence as I put my hand on the doorknob and slowly turned it. I had my finger firmly on the trigger, ready to blaze the whole fucking room.

I opened the door and a huge wooden table greeted me. In front of the table was the back of a woman's body. When my eyes focused and got a clearer look, I realized it was Maya. She was standing as if frozen in her space. I kept my gun aimed, prepared for any surprises. As I got closer, my vision captured the puddles of blood streaming across the floor. Then Maya felt a presence and turned towards me with her gun pointed in my direction.

"Maya, put the gun down," I said calmly. The distant look on her face told me her mind wasn't all there. She appeared to be in shock. "Maya, put the gun down," I repeated, worried that she may accidentally pull that trigger and I would have to take her out on some it's-my-life-over-yours type shit. To my relief, it seemed things were clicking and she laid the gun down on top of the table.

"I didn't have a choice, Precious. She was gonna kill me," Maya said, sounding stunned by whatever just took place.

After making my way from around the table and with nothing obscuring my sight, that's when the dead bodies welcomed me. Lying face up were Clip and Destiny. I couldn't believe it, another brick wall. With both Clip and Destiny dead, we would get no answers. In my desperation, I ran and bent down beside them to check their pulses, praying for a miracle. But there would be no miracle today; they had completely flat lined.

"Maya, what happened?" She remained unemotional, not saying a word.

Then we both jumped, startled by the blaring police sirens surrounding the building.

"Did you call the police?" Maya asked as fear seemed to take her over.

"No, I called Supreme when I got here. I was worried about you. He must've told Detective Moore what was going on and they brought the whole fucking army with them."

"Oh fuck, Precious, I don't want to go to jail. It was self defense… I didn't have a choice… it was either kill or be killed. It was Clip. Precious, he's the one that's responsible for helping Mike kidnap Aaliyah," she said in bewilderment.

"Maya," I said, standing up and holding her hand, hoping to snap her out of her daze. "How did you find out about Clip? Did he tell you where Mike has Aaliyah? I need you to concentrate, Maya."

"Drop your weapons and put your hands up!" the police yelled. There were about twenty of those motherfuckas armed with enough artillery to take out a small country.

I had flashbacks to when the cops swarmed Mike's house after he raped me, then Supreme busted in and I found out that he wasn't dead after all. I had never seen so many damn cops… until now. I don't give a fuck what anybody says, having a slew of guns aimed in your face with crackers dying to pull the trigger will make even the hardest badass want to piss in their pants. That's why with the quickness I put my gun down on top of the table next to Maya's weapon and put my hands up.

"Mrs. Mills, are you okay?" Detective Moore asked, making his way through the crowd of officers. I had never been so stoked to see his irritating ass, I almost bust a smile.

"I'm cool, but I'll be better if you could get your men to lower their weapons. They're not in any threat, and ain't anybody else here." The officers still didn't budge, making it clear my words didn't mean shit.

"Is there anybody down?" Detective Moore wanted to know. I assumed he meant dead people.

"Yes, two," I answered, looking down at Clip and Destiny.

Detective Moore walked towards the scene with his weapon raised and observed the dead bodies. He checked their pulses and then stood up, retrieving my gun and Maya's off the table.

"You can put your weapons down," he finally ordered the other cops.

No longer feeling like a criminal, I put my hands down and relaxed. "Where's Supreme?"

"He's outside. This is a crime scene so they can't let him in." Detective Moore then reached inside his suit jacket and pulled out a pad and pen. "I need to take a statement. Who wants to go first?" Detective Moore instantly jumped to business as usual.

"I will," Maya said, leaning against the table.

I put my hand up. "Hold on, Maya. I think we should wait for our attorney before answering any of your questions... no offense to you, Detective Moore."

He gave me a smug stare, but I played the cops and robbers game enough times to know better.

"Precious, I have nothing to hide. I want to tell you what happened."

"I don't think that's a good idea."

"Mrs. Mills, if your friend wants to talk, then I think you should let her. All we want is to get to the truth. It might even help us with our investigation regarding the whereabouts of your daughter."

"Detective Moore, don't use my daughter as bait to get Maya to talk."

"That's not what I'm doing. I was simply..."

Maya cut him off mid-sentence. "Please, stop. Precious, I want to talk. Like I said, I have nothing to hide."

"Then go 'head," I said, tired of going back and forth with it.

Detective Moore's beady blue eyes pierced in on Maya, as he was ready to hang onto her every word.

"Earlier today I went to the apartment and met up with Clip. We were trying to patch things up after I had found out he was screwing around on me with that Destiny chick."

"And Destiny, that's the deceased who's lying next

to your boyfriend?" Detective Moore double-checked before jotting it down on his pad.

"Yes. He was finally admitting what had been going on between them, and swore that it was over and he wanted a chance to work things out between us. I agreed. I was in love with him. So we engaged in some make-up sex and I fell asleep. When I woke up, I overheard him talking to someone on the phone in the living room, so I went in the bedroom and picked up the phone to eavesdrop. He was talking to Destiny. She was threatening him, saying that if he didn't meet her she would go to the cops and his life would be over."

"What did she have on him?" the detective inquired, as if he wanted to know more for his own personal pleasure than a homicide investigation.

"She didn't say, but obviously he knew what she was speaking of because he agreed to meet her. She gave him the address and I also wrote it down. A few minutes later, he came in the room and said he had to go to the studio and work on some things, and that he would be back in a couple of hours. Of course I knew he was lying, but I didn't say anything. I wanted to get to the truth, and he wasn't going to tell me so I decided to find out my own way.

"After he left, I got dressed and headed here. I stopped at a pay phone and called Precious when I got close because I didn't know what to expect."

"When you say you didn't know what to expect... in terms of what?"

"I mean, Detective, I'm from the streets. I wasn't sure

if I was gon' end up beating her ass for fucking around with my man or what. So I wanted to make sure I had my girl with me just in case she had brought some of her girlfriends with her. They coulda tried to tag team me. I needed backup."

I put my hands on Maya's shoulders. "Calm down, its okay," I said as she started getting extra amped up.

"I'm sorry."

"That's okay, Ms. Owens, continue."

"So, umm, after I placed the call to Precious, I came here and saw their cars parked in the back. I sneaked inside so I could try and hear their conversation because I wanted to know what Destiny had on Clip, and I…" Maya then let out a gasp, broke down and started crying.

"Maya, you'll be okay," I said, holding her up, so she wouldn't fall down.

"Would you like to sit down, Ms. Owens? Officer, bring us that chair in the corner."

"I'm fine… I'm so sorry, this is harder than I thought it would be."

The officer brought Maya a chair and she sat down and got her bearings together. I was glad she sat down because the paramedics were now carrying off Clip in a body bag, and I knew how hard it was for her to see that.

"Let me know when you're ready to continue, Ms. Owens."

"I'm ready. So when I came inside, they were arguing. Destiny told Clip she had enough of the bullshitting and wanted the money he owed her. He told her the money was in his car. She said that was cool, but she wanted an extra hundred grand. He told her she was fucking crazy and that if she wanted anymore money that she would have to get it from Mike."

"Mike? Do you mean your brother, Mr. Owens?" Detective Moore stopped writing, waiting for her answer.

"Yes. Precious, I'm so sorry, you were right. Clip was helping Mike. He did help him kidnap Aaliyah. I can't believe I was so stupid."

"It's not your fault."

"Yes it is. If only I had listened to you, maybe we could've stopped him."

"Not to interrupt, but Ms. Owens, what happened next?"

"Destiny wasn't trying to hear it. She said fuck him and Mike, that she wanted her money or she would go to Supreme and tell him that he was the one who helped Mike kidnap his daughter. That's when Clip lost it and smacked the shit out of her. He then grabbed her by the neck and started choking her. But Destiny came prepared. She reached in the back of her jeans and pulled out a gun and shot Clip multiple times. He fell to the ground, and she went in his pockets to get his car keys and wallet. I walked up on her from behind and startled her. She turned the gun on me, and there was a struggle and it went off. At first I didn't even realize she had been shot. It all happened so fast."

I held Maya tightly, as I could see the anguish in her eyes. I knew she hated Clip for what he had done, but she also loved him and no matter how horrible he was. She couldn't erase those feelings just like that.

"Detective Moore, I think you should come out here," one of the officers came up and said.

"Ladies, stay here, I'll be back right back."

I nodded my head and focused my attention back on Maya. Tears were streaming down her face and I knew there was nothing I could do to make her feel better.

"Precious, I feel so responsible."

"Why? You can't blame yourself for what Clip did."

"But it's like, first my brother rapes you, and now my boyfriend helped him make you and Supreme's life a living hell by kidnapping your daughter. How could I have had two monsters in my life and not know it?"

"You're not responsible for their actions."

"I wish I felt that way. And I wish I hadn't killed Destiny, because she probably knew where Aaliyah is. Now how are we going to find her?"

I didn't even try to answer that question, because I kept asking myself the same thing. For every two steps forward, it seemed we would take two steps back. I honestly didn't know how much more of this I could take.

"Mrs. Mills, Detective Moore wanted you to follow me," an officer came to inform me.

"Now?"

"Yes, he said it's important."

"Maya, do you want to stay here or come with me?"

"I'll come with you."

Maya and I followed the officer out the back door. There were dozens of police cars and news crews. I could hardly see as I was blinded by the lights coming from the cameras. The officer had to push through the hordes of people.

"What the fuck is going on? Get these people out the

way!" I complained. When we finally broke through the crowd, I saw Detective Moore standing in front of what appeared to be Supreme. "Oh shit, what the fuck is he harassing Supreme about?" I said, sick of being pestered by the cops. Due to the growing crowd, it took a few more minutes for us to make our way to Supreme and the detective. But when we did, I had to grab a hold of the officer in front of me so I wouldn't bust my ass falling down. My mouth dropped and the tears flowed.

"Precious, what's wrong?" Maya called out, unable to see what I could because I was blocking what was in front of me.

"I can't believe this… this can't be real!" I screamed out.

Supreme heard my voice and turned his body towards mine. "Yes it is," he said, coming towards me. My heart wouldn't let me believe it until I locked it in. There Supreme stood, cradling our baby.

"Aaliyah, my baby!" I put my head down and couldn't stop crying. She was bundled up in blankets, and I extended my arms out so I could hold her. Her eyes were closed, but when he put her in my arms and I held her, she opened them. The beautiful eyes she inherited from her grandmother welcomed me with open arms. I put her to my chest and held her so tightly. "You're home. My baby is finally home." Supreme wrapped his arms around me, and all I could do was thank God for what I called a miracle.

"I told you we would bring your baby home," Detective Moore boasted.

I didn't know if I wanted to punch him or hug him.

"Where was she?" I wanted to know.

"Buckled up in the back seat of that truck."

"She was here the whole time?" I couldn't believe it.

"Yes, we had no idea she was in there. With the dark tint on the car and how it's parked, we had no way of seeing her. The baby must've been asleep and finally woke up because one of the officers heard crying coming from the vehicle. All of us were overjoyed it turned out to be your child."

"Thank you, Detective. I mean that from the bottom of my heart."

"I appreciate that, Mrs. Mills. I know you don't want to part from you daughter, but we need to take her to the hospital and have her examined by a doctor. The paramedics did check her out... but you understand."

"Of course I understand, as long as you understand that I'll be taking that ride with her to the hospital. I won't be leaving her side anytime soon."

"Precious, Supreme, I'm so happy for both of you," Maya said, staring down at Aaliyah. "I guess things turned out okay after all."

"And we have you to thank for that, Maya," I said.

"Me? Why are you thanking me?"

"Because if you hadn't decided to follow Clip and see what the hell was going on, we would've never found this place or our daughter. You're the one who deserves the credit for bringing Aaliyah home. I'll never forget what you've done."

"She's right, Maya. Thank you. I know you lost Clip, but you helped us get back our daughter," Supreme said, giving Maya a hug.

As we stood in the parking lot and I held my precious daughter for the first time in so long, I was overcome with true happiness. I was surrounded by the only real family I had ever known. If I had learned one thing from this entire situation, it was that you have to appreciate your time with the ones you love and never take it for granted, because life is much too sacred. Once again I had been given another chance in life to make things better, and I planned on doing exactly that.

LIGHTS OUT

"Happy Birthday, Aaliyah!" we hummed in unison. I couldn't believe that Aaliyah was one year old already. It seemed like yesterday I was in the hospital, knocking on death's door pushing her out, and now she was walking and trying to talk. I felt so blessed that I was able to witness those milestones. After bringing Aaliyah home, the last three months had been such an adjustment. Supreme and I were both guilty of damn near suffocating her with our attention. We still hadn't accepted there was no making up for lost time.

"Aaliyah, Mommy loves you, baby," I said, squeezing her tightly. She looked simply delicious in her ruby-red Grace attire. The velvet dress with silk trim and bow detail made her look like a little princess.

"Supreme, you stand in the middle so I can take a picture of the three of you," Maya said, holding her digital camera. "One, two, three, say cheese."

"Che-e-e-e-se!"

Aaliyah had the biggest grin on her face as the camera snapped, loving the attention. Aaliyah snuggled in her daddy's arms, now demanding all of his adoration.

"That was perfect. You guys really are the first family of hip hop royalty. Now only if I can find me a man," Maya said as we walked towards the gazebo.

"Maya, when the time is right you will find a man. You've been through a lot. You need to focus on you, and everything else will come."

"That's easy for you to say. You have Supreme and the most beautiful little girl in the world. What do I have?"

"You have us."

"Come on, Precious. I can't live under your roof forever. Eventually I have to get out on my own.'

"Nobody is rushing you. Now that the police investigation is closed and the prosecution won't be bringing any charges against you, you need some time to fall back and relax."

"It's still hard to believe that Clip is gone. I know what he did was fucked up, but I loved him and I never thought he could be capable of anything like that."

"You're not the only one. He fooled Supreme too. He won't admit it, but he's hurting over what Clip did. He had a lot love for him. That was his protégé. Clip was going to be the next big rap phenomenon, and now he refuses to release his album even though it's completed. Supreme said any profits made off that CD would be blood money. He doesn't even care that he invested millions of dollars, and all that money has now gone to waste. But I recognize where Supreme is coming from."

"So do I. Plus, it don't help matters that Mike is out there somewhere."

"Who you telling? It's like he's vanished into thin air. Every lead on him comes up cold. The last time we talked to Detective Moore he said that there was a sighting of him in New Mexico, but after that, *nada*. I won't feel completely safe until he's captured and back behind bars."

"I know, but with all the help he had on the outside dead, I have a feeling his time on the run will be coming to an end shortly."

"That's what the detective believes too. But enough about Mike's sorry ass. Today is one of celebration and I'm not going to let that sick fuck rain on our parade. I'd rather discuss how much we love having you here with us, and how wonderful you are with Aaliyah."

"I love being here too, especially since you guys are the only family I have. I mean I could always go back to New York and live with my mother, but you know what a headache that was. But with you bringing Anna back, you're not going to need me anymore."

"First of all, I'm not even sure if Anna will agree to come back. Just because she was willing to attend Aaliyah's birthday party doesn't mean she wants to work for me again, and honestly I couldn't blame her."

"Precious, I'm sure Anna understands that you were only reacting to the fucked up events that took place. I mean, your daughter was kidnapped and she was the last person with her. It's only natural you would take your frustrations out on her."

"Regardless, whether Anna comes back or not, that doesn't have anything to do with whether you stay or go. Like I said, you're welcome to live here for as long as you want. I actually enjoy your company. You know I don't really like fucking with these uppity Beverly Hills motherfuckas. You're the only friend I got," I laughed.

As Maya and I sat down under the gazebo, I watched everyone enjoying the festivities. What started off being a few close friends and family turned into quite an event. But they were mostly all Supreme's people. His parents came and damn near all his industry friends who had kids, and even the ones who didn't. I had never seen so many baby mamas in one vicinity in all my life. This was the life of the "rich and shameless".

"Well, girl, these mofos have been at my house long enough. It's time to clear house. The party is officially over. Do you care to join me as I kick these motherfuckas out?" I joked, but was dead serious.

"Of course. Lead the way." By the time Maya and I blew the last kiss goodbye to my fellow guests, not only was it way past Aaliyah's bedtime, but I was exhausted. The only thing I wanted to do was crawl into bed with my husband and get some good loving.

"Baby, I'ma put Aaliyah to bed," Supreme said, holding our daughter in his arms.

Her eyes were closed so I gave her a soft kiss on the cheek so I wouldn't wake her up. I stood in the middle of the living room smiling, watching Supreme carry Aaliyah upstairs, feeling that my life couldn't get any better than this.

"Mrs. Mills, which room would you like for me to sleep in tonight?" Anna asked while I stood in the foyer captivated by the bond between Aaliyah and Supreme. It was a connection I never shared with my own father, a man I never even knew.

"I'm sorry, Anna what did you say?" I asked, coming out of my daydreaming.

"What room should I sleep in?"

"Your old room, but only if you agree to stay, Anna." I gave her a pleading look, hoping she would take me up on my offer.

"You really want me to come back and work for you, Mrs. Mills?" she asked with complete astonishment in her voice.

"Yes. I understand if you have reservations. I mean I treated you pretty badly. I was happy you agreed to come join us for Aaliyah's birthday party, although I figured it was because Supreme asked you."

"You know how highly I think of Mr. Mills, but I think highly of you too, Mrs. Mills and I also love baby Aaliyah very much. Nothing would make me happier than to be a part of your family again."

"Thank you, Anna," I said as we embraced. "Things are finally getting back to normal."

With everybody gone, and with both Anna and Maya tucked away in their rooms, I made a pit stop to the kitchen. I pulled out an ice cold bottle of bubbly for me and my husband. With two champagne glasses, whipped cream and strawberries in my hands I made my way to our bedroom, ready for us to toast the night away.

"What is all this?" Supreme asked as I entered our bedroom.

"I thought that since the kids played all day, it was time for the grown folks to do a little celebrating."

"What did you have in mind?"

"Some champagne, and then you rocking me to sleep. How does that sound?"

"Sounds tempting, but, umm…"

"But umm… what?"

"You want me to rock you to sleep, that means I have to do all the work. Shouldn't there be some sort of even exchange?"

"Excuse me?"

"No need to get hostile, all I'm saying is that can't you show me a little gratitude for all the work I'm about to put in?"

"A little gratitude… I think I can do that."

"I appreciate the cooperation, but first, can you take your clothes off? Gratitude is so much more fulfilling when you're naked." Neither of us could hold back our laughter.

"You're a mess, but your wish is my command." After placing our goodies on the nightstand beside the bed, I untied my midnight-blue Diane Von Furstenberg wrap dress. Then off came the laciest black La Perla bra and panty set. By the time I was done, the only thing left on me was my jewel-studded Giuseppe stilettos."

"Now that's more like it."

"Does that mean you're feeling the gratitude?" I flirted.

"You're getting there."

"Aren't you a hard one to please? I have a feeling this will do the trick, but first let's have a toast," I said, pouring champagne in our glasses. I put my hand around the necklace Supreme gave me in the hospital after surviving my brush with death. I turned over the pink diamond heart-shaped necklace, "You see that? It says 'S&P Love for Life'. That's you and me, baby. Can't nothing come between that."

"Let's toast to S&P Love for Life. You're the only woman for me, and I better be the only man for you," Supreme said, pulling me into a deep kiss. We clinked our glasses and drank up the champagne, solidifying our toast.

After tasting Supreme's lips, I continued sprinkling kisses down each crest of his chiseled chest, then stopped, using the tip of my tongue to circle his belly button. As his eyes rolled in delight, I took the whipped cream and polished his manhood, devouring each inch of him until he was ready to explode in my mouth. When he seemed as if he couldn't hold back any longer, I began to straddle him, and his dick penetrated inside of me.

"Damn, baby, my pussy feels so good!" he moaned, and pulled my breasts to his mouth.

I closed my eyes, winding my hips like I was a belly dancer. Warmth encompassed my insides as my first orgasm set upon me. "Supreme, don't ever leave me."

"I ain't going nowhere, just as long as you don't ever leave me."

"I'll never leave you. I promise you that." And as our

bodies became interwoven I meant every word I said. Supreme was it for me. There was no greater love than the one we shared together.

That night, Supreme and I made love until we fell asleep in each other's arms. We had once again been through the fire, but we came out of it stronger and more bonded than ever. Our love continued to stand against every obstacle thrown our way. I guess it's true what they say: "There's no greater love than Black love."

"Good morning, baby," I said, giving Supreme a kiss on the lips.

"Good morning to you. Last night was incredible. I fell in love with you all over again."

"Damn, I need to pull out the whipped cream more often."

"Yeah, you should."

"Don't be cute," I teased, tossing a pillow over his face.

"Oh, so now you want to play. I hear a pillow fight."

"No, no, no. I don't have the time for that. I'ma have to take a rain check," I said, jumping out of bed.

"Where are you off to?"

"First the shower, then after that it's a surprise."

"A surprise for who?"

"A surprise for my husband."

A gigantic smile lit up Supreme's face.

"You have a surprise for me? What is it?"

"Supreme, if I told you what it was, then it wouldn't be a surprise, now would it?"

"So you have to leave the house to get it?"

"Ye-e-e-e-s-s-s-s!"

"Okay, okay. You got me all excited like I'm a little kid at Christmas. I don't know what I'm going to do with myself until you get back."

"I'm sure you'll think of something."

"Already have. I'll take Aaliyah in the back and play roll-the-ball. Don't ask me why, but she gets the biggest kick outta that."

"Great. And by the way, Anna has agreed to come back and work for us again."

"That's what's up!"

"I thought for sure I was going to have to send you in to beg her to return, but she didn't make me grovel."

"Anna's good people, but stop talking to me. Go get ready so you can hurry up and come back with my surprise."

"You really are acting like a big kid, but I love you so it doesn't matter. I'm off," I said, disappearing to the shower.

As the hot water splashed against my body, I decided that I would plan a family trip for me, Supreme and Aaliyah. The three of us would go to some exotic island and have quality time together away from LA and the hectic schedule that Supreme was susceptible to on a regular basis. So, the jewelry I was picking up for Supreme would only be the first part of the surprise, and our family trip would be part two.

By the time I got out of the shower, Supreme had already left the room and I assumed he was somewhere tickling Aaliyah, since that's what he loved to do first thing every morning. After getting dressed, I stopped by Maya's room to see if she wanted to take a ride with me to the jewelry store. I knocked on her door but got no answer, so I opened the door to see if she was still asleep. "Maya," I called out, thinking maybe she was in her bathroom, but I got no answer. "Maybe she's downstairs," I said and closed the door back.

When I got downstairs the house was already lively. Supreme and Aaliyah were sitting on the living room sofa, and I could smell the aroma of scrumptious food coming from the kitchen, and knew it had to be Anna in there whipping up one of her to-die-for meals. Then Aaliyah saw me and rolled off the sofa and ran towards me with her arms out. "Hi, my baby. Mommy missed you," I said, picking her up and swinging her around. Aaliyah put her head back and laughed her little heart out.

"Listen, Mommy has to go now because I have to go get a special surprise for your Daddy. But I'll be back soon, so keep Big Papa entertained until I return." I nuzzled my nose against her neck and she laughed even harder.

"Come here, little girl. Come play with Daddy until your Mommy gets back," Supreme said, taking Aaliyah out my arms and lifting her in the air. "Now you hurry back."

"I will. Oh, by the way, have you seen Maya?"

"No, I assumed she was in her room still sleep."

"No, I checked but she was gone. Maybe she had something to do early this morning. I'll call her when I get in the car."

"Do you want me to have someone drive you?"

"That's okay, I'm good. Plus, I want to take your new Lamborghini for a spin."

"Oh really now?"

"Yes, really. I know it's parked right outside. That's why I was looking for Maya. Two hot chicks in that whip, can you imagine all the men we could pick up? I'm only joking, so get that frown off your face."

"Your mother trying to make Daddy lose it up in here," Supreme said to Aaliyah as if she understood exactly what he was saying.

"Bye, you guys. I'll see you in a little bit."

Supreme and Aaliyah walked me to the door and waved goodbye as I got in the car. I put the key in the ignition and clutched my hand on the stick shift, speeding off with the morning sun shining brightly. I had Nas blazing through the speakers, and I was caught up in my own groove, oblivious to world around me. It was like that the entire time until I pulled up to the Cartier store on Rodeo Drive. Arriving first thing in the morning before the streets turned into the who's who of Hollywood, I stepped out of my car high off the notion of how fucking incredible my life was.

As I was about to exit Supreme's custom shocking-pink Genaddi Lamborghini Murcielgo Roadster, I heard my cell. I didn't recognize the number but opted to answer anyway. "Hello?"

"Hi, Precious, I'm happy for you and your family. I wanted to call sooner, but I knew you and Supreme would want some time alone after bringing your daughter home."

"Nico, thank you so much. I'm glad that you called," I said, stepping out of the car. "I was wondering if I would hear from you again. I…"

"Precious, are you there?"

I heard Nico's voice but my response lingered in the air. Out of nowhere, the black tinted SUV seemed to appear like a dark cloud before the storm. I had no preparation as my body was lifted off the ground, causing me to drop my phone. I could still hear Nico screaming out my name as it hit the pavement. I was thrown into the truck, and before I could utter a word or fight back, the wet cloth with chloroform knocked me out, lickety-split.

"So we meet again. I knew we would. I've been waiting for this day for a very long time."

My eyes couldn't focus on the figure standing in front of me. I could hear a voice, but I was struggling to get out of the chloroform-induced daze.

"Wake up," the voice demanded as a hand gripped my chin. But I was finding it impossible to center my attention until a punch landed on my jaw, causing my head to rock to the side.

"Who the fuck are you and what do you want from me?" I mumbled, feeling as if my head was about to fall off my neck.

"Oh, you don't know who the fuck I am? Look real closely."

My central vision was coming back, but as soon as it did I wanted it to vanish. The image in front of me was too devastating to believe.

"Mike, you had to come back." His head was completely bald but the eyes never lie, and it was him, Pretty Boy Mike in the flesh.

"Hmm, that's the thing. I never left. I was waiting for the right time for you to put your guard down. Take a look around, because this will be your new home for a very long time," he said, spreading out his arms. He was wearing a three-piece suit and looking like a hood version of Creflo Dollar.

I scanned the room and it looked like I was in a dreary basement of a house. It was cold and had no windows. I was on the floor, with both my hands and legs tied up to a pipe. "You just don't know when to stop. I thought after Clip got killed helping out your sick ass you would've crawled under a rock and choked to death. But look at where I am now. Obviously I'm not that lucky," I spewed.

"Now, Precious, you know Clip didn't have enough balls to kidnap a puppy, let alone the baby of the great Supreme. You couldn't really believe that incompetent idiot had the brains to pull that off," another voice said from the shadows.

"Whoever said that, show your face right now!" I

commanded.

"Your ears aren't playing tricks on you," the voice stated, stepping into the light.

"You! I presume you truly are your brother's keeper."

"Yes, I am," Maya boasted.

"This was all a setup."

Maya and Mike started clapping. "But wait, we can't forget about the hard work Devon put in," Maya said as Devon then stepped into the light.

"I never did like your motherfuckin' ass," I growled at Devon.

"Then we have something in common. Before I put that bullet in Vernika, it took every ounce of me not to aim at you. But I was following orders so I had to let you live."

"So you three clowns orchestrated this whole thing. Unfuckin' believable."

"Dear brother, I think I should get most of the credit. It was me who hired that dumb Destiny to make it look as if she was cheating with my man."

"What do you mean, look as if he was cheating? I caught them in…" There was no need to complete my thought, as all the pieces popped in my head and came together at once. "You conniving bitch, you set it up for me to find Clip and Destiny together. That's why he seemed so out of it when he woke up. You scandalous hoes' drugged his ass."

"Without a doubt. It started the day you came over and I put that bug in your ear about the crank phone calls I was getting at the house and the missing money that

Clip couldn't account for. Then I made sure when we went to the video shoot that you caught Destiny coming out of Clip's room, you know, just to start raising doubt. Then that day I conveniently had you pick me up from the car dealership, I had already drugged Clip, and Destiny was at my place waiting for my phone call so she could put our plan in action. From the moment you caught him and Destiny in bed together, nothing could dissuade your belief that Clip was not only a cheat, but Mike's accomplice."

"Clip had absolutely nothing to do with any of this, and after using him as your fall guy you killed him?"

"Pretty much. But unfortunately I can't take credit for killing Clip. Destiny did that dirty deed for me. After you and Supreme managed to get the address to where Donnell and Vernika were staying, I knew we had to act fast. It was only a matter of time before you would find the apartment that I had Destiny staying at with Aaliyah. But of course I had to leave just enough evidence to implicate Clip without jumping overboard."

"You're feeling real proud of yourself, aren't you, Maya? You're even crazier than your fuckin' deranged brother."

"Why thank you. But let me finish." Maya smiled, showing how swollen with pride she was of her accomplishments. "It was time to cut off all loose ends. So Devon went back after his shift and finished off Chris and Donnell. Then dumbass Destiny believed she was meeting me at the warehouse to give me Aaliyah, kill clueless Clip and collect a shit-load of money. Up until

I put that bullet in her, she had no idea that her services were no longer needed and her time was up. And poor Clip, he thought he was coming to the warehouse to save me. He was devastated when I laughed in his face and told him he was nothing but a pawn in my deadly game."

"I'm impressed, Maya. If it wasn't for your diligence, none of this would be possible," Mike said, patting his younger sister on the back of her shoulder.

"So, Maya, you never loved Clip. It was always your plan to use him as a cover-up to get your brother out of jail, and then what? What is your ultimate goal, to kill me? Then go ahead and do it."

"We can always count on you to be tough as nails to the bitter end, can't we, Precious?" Mike scolded.

"Let me handle this, Mike," Maya said, hushing her brother and making it clear that she was the one running the show. "I had been secretly talking to my brother for a very long time. I hated you for sending him to prison. He was the only real family I had. Nobody gave a fuck about me, including my mother. Mike was the only person who took care of me."

"How soon we forget. I took care of you, Maya. I treated you like my very own sister and this is how you repay me?"

"Get the fuck off your pedestal. You really think your shit don't stink. You took my brother away from me."

"He raped me and tried to kill Supreme. Putting him in a jail cell was a gift. He deserved to be buried alive."

"Whatever my brother did to you, you deserved it, and you were never good enough for a man like Supreme.

I'm the type of woman that can hold it down for him. I've decided I want Supreme for myself. I mean, why should I have to play second fiddle to you? Why should I have to be stuck with a wannabe like Clip? I deserve the king."

"Oh shit, here we go!" Mike growled.

"Dear brother, you know the deal. You get your freedom and I get my life with Supreme."

"You really are crazy. You will never have Supreme. He will see right through you."

"You didn't," Maya said mockingly. "Trust me, Supreme will be so heartbroken when you never come home that he'll seek the comfort from a dear friend like myself."

"Oh please! When Supreme realizes I'm dead he'll start putting the pieces together and point the finger right to your manipulating ass."

"By the time your dead, it'll be too late and it won't matter. See, I want you to be alive and have a front row seat as I take over your life. You'll watch as I make your husband fall in love with me, and your beautiful daughter, Aaliyah will be calling me Mommy."

"You'll never pull it off."

"You better hope I do, because if not, that little precious daughter of yours is going to end up dead."

"Maya, that might be my flesh and blood you're threatening to kill, and your niece," Mike reminded her, seeming genuinely stunned that Maya would make such a threat on Aaliyah.

"Mike, shut up. You're taking this Maury Povich, I-might-be-the-father thing way too far. If it wasn't for me, you wouldn't have thought for a second that Aaliyah might be your daughter, so save it."

"Now it makes sense. Your trifling ass was the one that made Mike feel so confident he was Aaliyah's father. I guess she was the perfect bait to wave in front of your brother's face so he would be a willing participant with this bullshit plan you're trying to pull off."

"I ain't trying to do shit! My eyes see very well, and from where I'm standing, your ass is on lock and I'm the one who is free, about to go to the crib you used to share with Supreme and comfort him. So the bullshit plan you're speaking of has been pulled off as far as I'm concerned."

"Maya, you better kill me now, because if I ever get free…" my voice faded off.

"I so admire your fire. It's contagious. Here, I brought this for you to keep your heart warm at night." Maya pulled out something from her pocket and handed it to me. "I thought it was only fair you have it, since it's the last picture you will ever take with your family."

It was the photo of me, Supreme, and Aaliyah that Maya took yesterday at her birthday party. I fought back the tear that wanted to escape my eye. This couldn't be it for me. The happiest moment of my life, ripped from me just like that. "I swear you're gonna pay for this, Maya. I put that on everything I love."

"Precious, save your threats. It's lights out for you. Bow down, I'm the new queen bitch."

IN STORES NOW

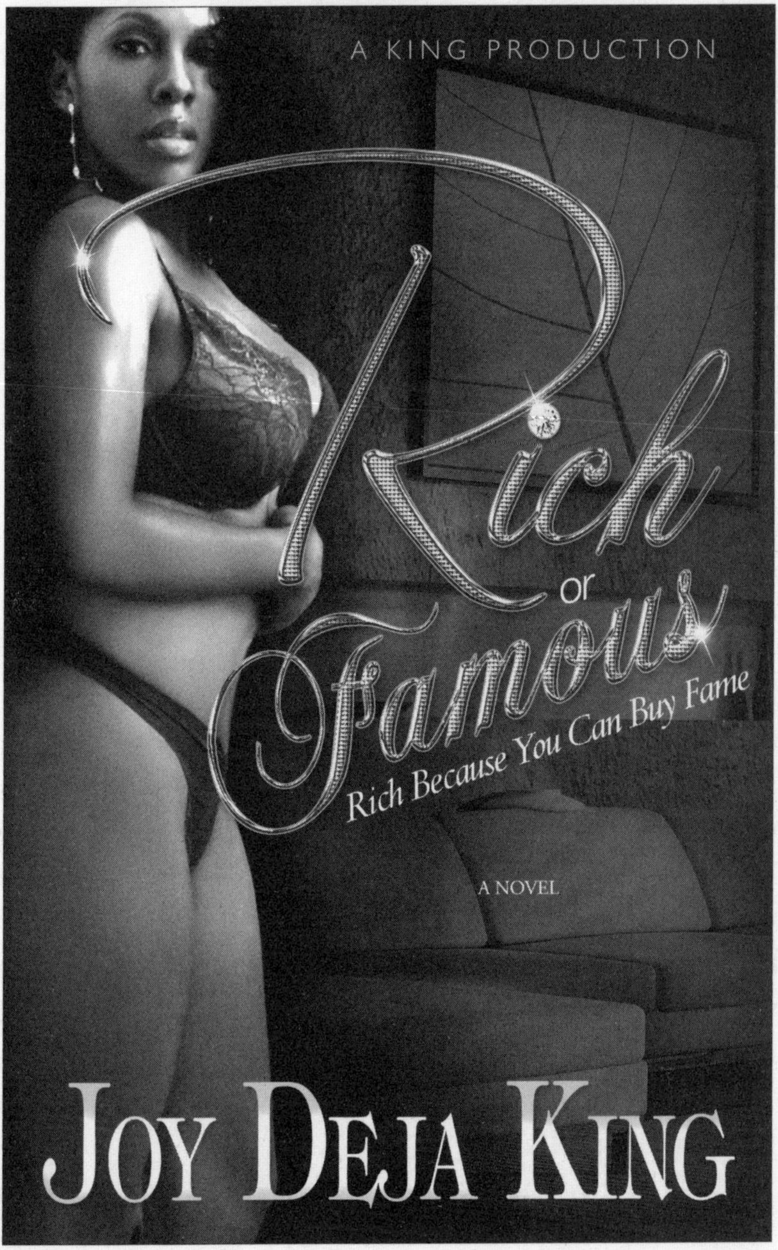

Lorenzo

Welcome To My World

★★★★★

Before I die, if you don't remember anything else I ever taught you, know this. A man will be judged, not on what he has but how much of it. So you find a way to make money and when you think you've made enough, make some more, because you'll need it to survive in this cruel world. Money will be the only thing to save you. As I sat across from Darnell those words my father said to me on his deathbed played in my head.

"Yo, Lorenzo, are you listening to me, did you hear anything I said?"

"I heard everything you said. The problem

for you is I don't give a fuck." I responded, giving a casual shoulder shrug as I rested my thumb under my chin with my index finger above my mouth.

"What you mean, you don't give a fuck? We been doing business for over three years now and that's the best you got for me?"

"Here's the thing, Darnell, I got informants all over these streets. As a matter of fact that broad you've had in your back pocket for the last few weeks is one of them."

"I don't understand what you saying," Darnell said swallowing hard. He tried to keep the tone of his voice calm, but his body composure was speaking something different.

"Alexus, has earned every dollar I've paid her to fuck wit' yo' blood suckin' ass. You a fake fuck wit' no fangs. You wanna play wit' my 100 g's like you at the casino. That's a real dummy move, Darnell." I could see the sweat beads gathering, resting in the creases of Darnell's forehead.

"Lorenzo, man, I don't know what that bitch told you but none of it is true! I swear 'bout four niggas ran up in my crib last night and took all my shit. Now that I think about it, that trifling ho Alexus probably had me set up! She fucked us both over!"

I shook my head for a few seconds not believing this muthafucker was saying that shit with a straight face. "I thought you said it was two niggas that ran up in your crib now that shit done doubled.

Next thing you gon' spit is that all of Marcy projects was in on the stickup."

"Man, I can get your money. I can have it to you first thing tomorrow. I swear!"

"The thing is I need my money right now." I casually stood up from my seat and walked towards Darnell who now looked like he had been dipped in water. Watching him fall apart in front of my eyes made up for the fact that I would never get back a dime of the money he owed me.

"Zo, you so paid, this shit ain't gon' even faze you. All I'm asking for is less than twenty-four hours. You can at least give me that," Darnell pleaded.

"See, that's your first mistake, counting my pockets. My money is *my* money, so yes this shit do faze me."

"I didn't mean it like that. I wasn't tryna disrespect you. By this time tomorrow you will have your money and we can put this shit behind us." Darnell's eyes darted around in every direction instead of looking directly at me. A good liar, he was not.

"Since you were robbed of the money you owe me and the rest of my drugs, how you gon' get me my dough? I mean the way you tell it, they didn't leave you wit' nothin' but yo' dirty draws."

"I'll work it out. Don't even stress yourself, I got you, man."

"What you saying is that the nigga you so called

aligned yourself with, by using my money and my product, is going to hand it back over to you?"

"Zo, what you talking 'bout? I ain't aligned myself wit' nobody. That slaw ass bitch Alexus feeding you lies."

"No, that's you feeding me lies. Why don't you admit you no longer wanted to work for me? You felt you was big shit and could be your own boss. So you used my money and product to buy your way in with this other nigga to step in my territory. But you ain't no boss you a poser. And your need to perpetrate a fraud is going to cost you your life."

"Lorenzo, don't do this man! This is all a big misunderstanding. I swear on my daughter I will have your money tomorrow. Fuck, if you let me leave right now I'll have that shit to you tonight!" I listened to Darnell stutter his words.

My men, who had been patiently waiting in each corner of the warehouse, dressed in all black, loaded with nothing but artillery, stepped out of the darkness ready to obliterate the enemy I had once considered my best worker. Darnell's eyes widened as he witnessed the men who had saved and protected him on numerous occasions, as he dealt with the vultures he encountered in the street life, now ready to end his.

"Don't do this, Zo! Pleeease," Darnell was now on his knees begging.

"Damn, nigga, you already a thief and a back-stabber. Don't add, going out crying like a bitch to that too. Man the fuck up. At least take this bullet like a soldier."

"I'm sorry, Zo. Please don't do this. I gotta daughter that need me. Pleeease man, I'll do anything. Just don't kill me." The tears were pouring down Darnell's face and instead of softening me up it just made me even more pissed at his punk ass.

"Save your fuckin' tears. You shoulda thought about your daughter before you stole from me. You're the worse sort of thief. I invite you into my home, I make you a part of my family and you steal from me, you plot against me. Your daughter doesn't need you. You have nothing to teach her."

My men each pulled out their gat ready to attack and I put my hand up motioning them to stop. For the first time since Darnell arrived, a calm gaze spread across his face.

"I knew you didn't have the heart to let them kill me, Zo. We've been through so much together. I mean you Tania's God Father. We bigger than this and we will get through it," Darnell said, halfway smiling as he began getting off his knees and standing up.

"You're right, I don't have the heart to let them kill you, I'ma do that shit myself." Darnell didn't even have a chance to let what I said resonate with him because I just sprayed that muthafucker like the piece of shit he was. "Clean this shit up," I said, stepping over Darnell's bullet ridden body as I made my exit.